THE Wonderful TIME OF THE YEAR

A PRIDE & PREJUDICE CHRISTMAS CAROL

Ney Mitch

THE WONDERFUL TIME OF THE YEAR
Copyright © 2025 by Ney Mitch

ISBN: 979-8-88653-441-2

Published by Satin Romance
An Imprint of Melange Books, LLC
White Bear Lake, MN 55110
www.satinromance.com

Published in the United States of America.

Cover Design by Caroline Andrus

Dedication & Author's Note

Come one, come all, for I welcome you, Reader.

Whatever merry time of the year, I hope 'as it is often put in Regency times', that I find you all in good health.

During this time, I dashed off a ghostly little book, in the spirit of two literary greats, who can say they marked similar times of history.

After all, how often is it known that Charles Dickens was born a year after Jane Austen first published 'Sense & Sensibility'?

This tale shall begin a little over a decade into the Victorian Era.

My apologies if the mixing of Jane Austen's epic tale and Charles Dickens's iconic Christmas novella has been combined before, by the pen of other authors. If this classical merging has already been done, I was completely unaware of it, and hope the reader understands that there was no attempt to copy what another, perhaps better author, could have already achieved.

That being said, I do hope that you all, who pick up this

story, finds something in it to enjoy, and does not put you out of humor. Important Note: there will be an Afterword at the conclusion of the book, if the reader is curious.

I dedicate this book to my parents, family, friends, and all who helped me publish this book. I would be lost without them.

And for you, who turns past this page and sojourns forth, you chose to believe in me and gave me a chance. Once more, you have saved my life, and I appreciate it.

Special thanks to my publisher, editor, cover artist, and all the readers who picked up this novel and gave it a chance, thanks so very much! This dedication is for you.

Prologue

Mr. Darcy's mother was dead, to begin with. There is no doubt whatever about that. The register of her burial was signed by the clergyman, the clerk, the undertaker, and the chief mourner, Darcy's father, signed it. And Darcy's father's name was good upon 'legacy', for anything he chose to put his hand to.

Mr. Darcy's mother, Anne Darcy, was dead as a doornail.

Naturally, when the young Mr. Darcy, still a boy, had lost his mother, it was when he was away at University at the tender and soft age of sixteen. Between the separation, and the knowledge of losing one of the best friends of his life, Darcy inwardly never accepted that he was not there at her very last moments in this world.

However, that did not render all the lessons that the late Mrs. Darcy taught him to be fruitless on her son's mind. On the contrary, her words, her mindset, and her heart had been thoroughly impressed on her son's opinions and attitude, and he believed that her word was now law.

After all, when given a devoted and adoring mother, what true son would not be considerate of her love and his learnings?

Yet, what could be said was that when he was informed, Darcy was ushered back home with all due course that could be described as quick, and he arrived in time for the funeral.

He saw the church filled with all the servants, his father, sister, and his mother's brother and sister. There were a small amount of other local families who had attended.

Yet, with Pemberley being such an illustrious home to the North, and being ten miles in diameter, it was not always easy to gather so many friends, because Mrs. Darcy did not often have many families close by.

At sixteen, Darcy stood next to his seven-year-old sister, Georgiana, who wept softly. Darcy naturally wished to cry himself.

He loved his mother to a vast degree and knew that there would be many days and many nights that he felt his mother deserved more time on this earth.

And that he deserved more of that time with her. Thus, he felt like a man incomplete, endured the length of his youth pulling away from him, and that he would have to grow up sooner than he would have wanted.

One could say that was when Fitzwilliam Darcy lost a lightness to his nature. And that lightness being gone tore away from his soul.

But his tale shall unfold as it may, for every man, like woman, has the right to speak for themselves, and have them walk down the road that they choose.

To continue, remembering the late Mrs. Darcy's funeral brings me back to the point that I started from. There is no doubt that Mrs. Darcy was dead.

This must be distinctly understood, or nothing wonderful can come from the story at this time of the year.

CHAPTER 1

The Young Sinner

"Unsupportable!" Darcy hissed as he was leaving his theatre box after watching a play at Drury Lane. When the show ended, Darcy didn't even applaud.

Between the nature of the play, and the lack of love that he had for that time of the year, he was not in the habit of finding joy in anything.

A handsome man of large fortune, a vast estate in the North and with a lovely townhouse in London would naturally make Mr. Fitzwilliam Darcy the perfect candidate for a man to marry.

Yet that would not be so, because time had rendered his best qualities into blandness, and his disappointments in life —disappointments that he had created from his own decisions—that it led to a sourness that crossed his features.

His handsome looks would quickly sink into plainness, because of the constant scowl that crossed it.

His lack of spark of life led to him drifting away from his friends, and soon every common acquaintance sank into a distant indifference. He had many in the ton who would invite him to parties, under the distinct impression that they would receive no reply.

Mr. Darcy had given up being social. People confused Darcy. And the word 'duty' became his chief frame of mind. But, soon that sense of duty came at a heavy price.

As such, when the play was finished, Darcy found the performance to be lackluster and there was nothing remarkable to see. He thought the acting was horrible, the leads were miscast, and that he had wasted his time.

As he left the box, there was an usher there to hold the door open for him to go downstairs.

"Did you enjoy the play, sir?" he asked.

"Not at all," Darcy said. "There was nothing to recommend it, this was a waste of effort and did nothing to elevate the typical story that it brings forth."

The usher raised an eyebrow, shocked by this harsh criticism.

"Oh, well, I am sorry that it did not suit you, sir."

"I am even more sorry that I decided to leave the comforts of my home to come to this dismal attempt at dramatization. Why I even come to see plays at all is tiresome. I ought to give it up entirely since it does nothing but give a poor representation of reality."

The usher was so overwhelmed by the man's harshness that all he could do was look away and mutter.

"Good evening, sir."

Darcy did not even respond but only put his hat back on and left Drury Lane.

~

As he emerged from the theatre, he was among those in his social circle. Those who did notice him gave him a gentle nod or pretended not to notice him altogether.

Lowering their voices, they spoke amongst themselves, wondering at the misanthrope that the Master of Pemberley had become.

"I know that he was always a little serious," a Mrs. Brownell said to her husband as they were waiting for a cabby. "But he turned into pure stone."

The wealthy widow, Mrs. Canby, who inherited Jellaby estate, stood with her son and gently moved her daughters to the side.

"Do not look at Mr. Darcy," Mrs. Canby whispered. "Never engage in discussion with him."

"But why, Mother?" their eldest daughter asked. "He looks handsome enough, and everyone says that he's rich."

"Rich and handsome is as rich and handsome does," the eldest son said, "to an extent. Penelope, I went to school with Darcy, and I can tell you that he went from serious at university to a state of worse every year. He's not worth catching or look at."

"And if he looks at you," the mother said, "his looks only find something wanting, and something to criticize and insult. Darcy likes being cruel and finds no woman good enough for him. He still hasn't even married the woman that he chose to marry."

Another set of gentlemen, one named Sir Marymoor, also whispered harsh words to his friend.

"Why does he even go out into society when he knows that he hates everything?"

All these questions, concerns, and remarks were unnoticed by Darcy. Even if they had not been spoken low, Darcy had reached such a disconnected disposition that he did not take heed of those around him, unless he could absolutely help it.

Internally, Darcy was dead, somewhat like a coffin nail.

Despite the lack of life that exuded from the dreadful Darcy fellow, it cannot be helped, nor prevented, that during his days, something would have no choice but to shock him.

Something to make him feel, to second-guess his mindset and manners.

Something to make him feel that thing called 'remorse'. And as he waited for his coach to be brought round from where it was parked, he heard a familiar voice from further down the way.

Through a large collection of people, he saw an old friend of his, being swarmed by a small crowd who were speaking to him. After all, despite being of the Novo riche, Mr. Charles Bingley was always a popular man.

When seeing him, Darcy blinked, and his expression shifted from intense stoicism to being slightly unnerved.

Three years!

That was the last time that he and Bingley spoke—the last time that they argued. And that argument cost Darcy a great deal. Marking his old friend, who was swarmed by others around him, Darcy was not wholly surprised that Bingley had many friends.

Being a solitary man, Darcy never regretted the loss of his social circle, but now, he felt strange.

Bingley was surrounded by many.

Darcy stood there alone.

And, surprisingly, Darcy felt something strange—something almost incredible: Darcy felt insecure.

However, Bingley had not gone to the theatre alone, for he rarely ever did any social event alone. Next to him, were his sisters, Caroline Bingley and Louisa Hurst. And while Bingley did not notice his distant friend, Caroline was good—rather she was expert—at observing her surroundings.

From the side of her eye, she glimpsed Mr. Darcy. Seeing her note him, Mr. Darcy whipped his head back towards the road, appearing preoccupied.

Still, he could see, from his peripheral perspective. He saw her tug at Charles Bingley's arm, and whisper that Darcy was near them.

He also saw how Bingley looked in his direction, and Bingley's eyes darkened with awkwardness and apathy, he said brief words to Caroline, showing that he was dismissive of the subject.

But Caroline Bingley was Caroline Bingley. Being the sort of person who liked pressing her point—as many of us have the desire to do—and she must've had a point to make.

After briefly arguing with her brother of him advising her to leave Darcy alone, Darcy saw Caroline approaching him.

Darcy's chest tightened, as he still looked ahead, and saw his carriage being brought round.

"Well," Caroline Bingley began, "Mr. Darcy, good evening."

"Good evening," Darcy said, tilting his head slightly and looking at her, without any emotion.

"It's been so long, but you have always been a busy man, since every invitation to my parties have been too inconvenient for you to attend."

"I find that parties no longer suit my palate."

"Well, they still suit me. After all, that is how I have found my fiancé."

When hearing that, Darcy looked at her with a raised eyebrow.

Any reaction at all was spice to the brew that Caroline had begun concocting because she dared hope to find jealousy in his eyes.

"Fiancé?" Darcy asked.

"Yes." Caroline gestured to a man who was standing near Bingley. The man was of a medium height, and Darcy found that the gentleman smiled too much. When analyzing the man's appearance, Darcy noticed that the man lacked a strong jaw, had a short forehead, indicating that he might not be the smartest man in the world. Especially since he did recognize him as Mr. John Hayter.

"John Hayter," Darcy uttered.

"Yes. I made his acquaintance at one of my parties, and who would have thought that would be one of the *happiest* moments of my life." Caroline stressed that last word, and Darcy knew why. He was hoping that this announcement would make him jealous. Especially since Darcy had always been aware of the soft feelings that Caroline had for him, back when they were tossed into each other's lives.

Unwilling to give her satisfaction, Darcy immediately lost all interest, and his gaze returned to apathy. Especially since he always found Mr. Hayter to be a very dull fellow who lacked anything like intelligence.

"I congratulate you," Darcy responded. "And I hope you both will be very happy."

Ever the keen observer, Darcy noted the disappointment in Caroline's eyes, and sadly, he reaped satisfaction from it.

"He is the perfect man for me," Caroline stressed, attempting to convince him of her success. "He has much conversation, and his rank and lifestyle work for my wealth. Now I know what true love is, and how we both feel it keenly."

"Love?" Darcy echoed.

"Yes, Mr. Darcy. We are in love."

Darcy rolled his eyes.

"I should have thought that there was more sense in that than love being the chief thing. But do as you will. Again, I congratulate you."

Caroline didn't know how to respond to it, because she was pained at seeing that she drew no warmth from him.

Naturally, she would want some sort of retaliation, and she was now giving it.

"I heard that you and Miss Anne de Bourgh had broken off your engagement. I am sorry that your life has not progressed."

Unaffected by his broken engagement, Darcy still had no reaction.

"It was for the best," Darcy responded curtly.

"How unfortunate! That some people just cannot find their happiness."

Darcy gave her a side glance.

"Have you really found your happiness, Caroline? Truly? Because I am not so certain."

"What proscription could you give instead?" Caroline asked, eager to know that he would mention himself as a potential suitor.

"Anyone but the one you chose," Darcy responded, "but do as you wish. It's not my business, nor my care."

Caroline's eyes filled with indignation.

"Good evening, Mr. Darcy," she said, her tone like ice. "And Merry Christmas."

"Quite frankly, I don't see anything merry about it."

"You wouldn't, would you?" she asked, then she turned her heel and rushed away, happy to be far from a man who she got no pleasure of ever saying the very thing that she wanted to hear.

Darcy's carriage came around, his servant helped him in, and Darcy rode off, leaving his one-time friends behind.

Despite himself, he did give a backwards glance at Charles Bingley, who had no choice but to watch Darcy's carriage roll down Broad Street, to the West End.

Looking through the window, Darcy saw pain in Bingley's eye, which Darcy understood but did not regret.

Bingley said that he would never forgive Darcy—and he never could. And Darcy never apologized because Darcy was never, in his eyes, wrong. Because, when it came to righteousness, Darcy was a tight-fisted hand at the obstinate. Hard and sharp as flint, he was, from which no steel had ever struck out generous fire.

Having once been a man who had developed great compassion, an open agreeable heart, Darcy's soul fell and shifted to being secret, self-contained, and solitary as an oyster.

CHAPTER 2

What Moved that Ought Not to Move

T he week leading up to Christmas Eve was uneventful for Darcy, but eventful for his staff.

Eager to get time to see their families, it was in their nature to ask for time away from Dover Street.

When Darcy had arrived at his townhouse on Christmas Eve, his butler, Mr. Hudson, met his master amiably. Darcy entered at 2 o'clock and confirmed what the cook made for dinner.

When Mr. Hudson confirmed all of this, apprehensively, Darcy walked up the steps, where he was met by his manservant, Mr. Jefferson.

Mr. Hudson gave Mr. Jefferson a look and Mr. Jefferson understood what that look meant.

He followed Mr. Darcy into his study and began to assist Mr. Darcy in removing his jacket and trousers and got him into his dressing gown, socks, and slippers.

"I have arranged a bath drawn for you, sir," Mr. Jefferson said, not expecting a reply, "and the fireplace's library has been lit for you to enjoy a good reading."

"Very well," Darcy replied, "and I thank you for not saying Merry Christmas to me. I can't abide hearing another person saying those two words to me, as if they have a right to be merry. Most of them are poor company, or poor in general. Even wealthy families today are scrounging around, jumping to marry their children off to anyone who has money, because they squandered their wealth. The world is always falling into chaos, and this society is going along with it."

"Yes, sir."

"Unsupportable! It's all unsupportable."

"Yes, sir."

Mr. Darcy removed his boots, handing them to Mr. Jefferson, who put them away.

"To know the correct way for the world to work, and to sit back and do nothing!"

"Yes, sir."

Mr. Hudson entered, informing Mr. Darcy that the bath was drawn. Mr. Jefferson said 'thank you' for Darcy, and Hudson did not leave.

Both Hudson and Jefferson were in alliance with each other, and they stood side by side while Darcy looked at himself in the mirror.

Seeing the two men standing together in his reflection, Darcy turned around.

"Is there a reason that you are still here, Hudson?" Darcy asked—more like he snapped.

"Forgive me, sir," Mr. Hudson said, a little unnerved. As the years rolled by, Mr. Hudson was an ideal servant who looked after the Darcy household well and fulfilled his duty as a butler to the best extent. Yet, he was never a forceful man, who never fully learned how to speak his words up sharp.

Fortunately, Mr. Jefferson was the reverse. Like Hudson, he too had served the Darcy family since the late Mr. Darcy was still alive. But being the personal servant to the father and son, it lent him more of an ability to approach delicate subjects without feeling as if he—what's the words for it—overstepped his authority.

"Pardon me, sir," Mr. Hudson began, "but tomorrow is Christmas Day."

"What of it?" Darcy asked, his tone stern.

"Well, it is customary for the staff to wish to see their families."

"Their families?" Darcy spat.

"Well," Mr. Hudson said, wiping his brow, nervous. "Yes, it is, sir."

"Master Darcy," Mr. Jefferson interjected, "Mr. Hudson and I have drafted the perfect staff plan where the staff can all leave this Christmas Eve, to stay with their families, and return the day after Christmas, without their being any disruption to your schedule."

"The whole day?" Mr. Darcy declared. "You are expecting that, all the servants, should be given the whole day off?"

"If it's quite convenient, sir," Mr. Hudson piped up.

"It is not convenient. And it's not fair to not have my entire staff fleeing from their duties at a time where I most require them. Yet I am quite certain that if I were to order otherwise, they all would feel ill-used. Would they not?"

"Sir," Mr. Jefferson said, "if I may, Mr. Hudson and I have arranged the staff plan so that, after dinner is served at six pm, Mr. Hudson and I shall remain for the duration of Christmas Eve. And on Christmas morning, Mr. Hudson shall leave, but I can remain."

"I have spoken to Mrs. Goodfellow," Mr. Hudson continued, "and, being such an excellent cook, she has prepared all meals that have rendered it easy for me to prepare myself. I do know how to master the ovens before I go to Tooley Street."

"Tooley Street," Darcy asked. "What is on Tooley Street?"

Mr. Jefferson and Mr. Hudson exchanged apprehensive looks.

"My family, sir. My family lives on Tooley Street."

Insensitive that he was to all this, as he was to all things regarding his servants' social lives, Darcy put on his dressing gown, to go to the washroom.

"I promise," Mr. Jefferson said, "there shall be no inconvenience of the kind, and I shall see that everything goes smoothly tonight and tomorrow."

"Very well," Darcy said, "tell the servants that they can take the day."

Mr. Hudson smiled and left to inform his staff downstairs.

In the washroom, Mr. Darcy slipped into the hot water in the tub as Mr. Jefferson prepared everything. While no earthly delights affected the stoic nature of the man, a bath was the contrary. In it, Darcy felt the soothing effects of being cleaned and made anew. This sensation, of feeling born again, did not go unnoticed by his manservant. Mr. Jefferson knew his master's hard ways, and in the brief activities that made that stern manner soften, for that was the best time to give him news.

As Jefferson handed Darcy a wash towel and his preferred soap and ointments, he informed his master that more hot water would be brought forth in a few minutes to warm the water again.

Darcy nodded, resting his head against the tub, and closing his eyes.

Soaked in water, Darcy cleaned off what he called 'the dirt of the day', in more ways than one. He did not simply remove the dirt, but he also was removing the world. For the comings and goings of the common folk, the ugly manners of the poor, the annoying desires of the middle class to aspire to better things, and the tedious nonsense of the wealthy, he could scarce display much, regarding them.

Gently, his mind drifted to when he saw Bingley and his sisters at the theatre. Rarely did he look back on his past in a manner which brought him pleasure. And seeing them all again was provocative because it did bring memories to the surface that he wanted to dismiss—and in turn, he wholly did.

For as was his way—the bath wiped away everything. Especially the remains of the day.

Bingley never forgave Darcy.

And Darcy never forgave Bingley for never forgiving him.

The parting of the ways had been sealed, and that relationship was over and done. As such, no more could be said on the subject to render Darcy into any attitude that could resemble that thing called: regret.

After a few minutes, Mr. Jefferson came in again with another bucket of hot water. Darcy leaned forward so that Jefferson could pour the hot water on his back and into the tub, warming the water even more.

The heat was refreshing, returning the bather to resting against the tub again as he cleaned himself.

Seeing his master in the best mood that he would wear, Mr. Jefferson stood there casually, not intimidated. After all, with his master, Jefferson learned that sounding meek was not endearing to Darcy. In fact, sounding comfortably confident appealed to Darcy more. Especially when it came to women. Jefferson knew—because Jefferson was there to see the woman that walked out of Darcy's life, and he was wrong to have lost.

"Master Darcy," Jefferson uttered, "since the staff shall be leaving after dinner, I think it best to give them their wages now. They shall need to purchase some food and presents for Christmas with their families."

"A full day's wages for not working," Darcy scoffed, "and they shall think of me as being the one who's ill-used when I pay a day's work to them. No doubt!"

"It is only once a year, and, if I may be so bold, servants to the Darcy family are of the highest caliber."

"You speak well for your fellow employees."

Jefferson blinked.

"They are my friends," he replied to his master, simply.

"Also, servants in this household are an ancient race where there are many of us. Often, I hear tales of servants not getting along with other servants in a household and constant arguments ensue. That can be disruptive to the running of things, but not here. I rarely ever argue with any of the staff, so I count my blessings. The twenty-fifth of December is a great day for them."

"But not for yourself?"

"I have no family to go to, but they do. Would you like me to distribute their wages for you, so to not put you through the trouble?"

"That is suitable."

"Very good, sir. Also, there were the usual letters of invitations for this time of the year."

"And you have written the polite responses that declined them?"

"I have, sir. Would you like to read them?"

"I will, after dinner."

"But there was one letter that I think will bring you some satisfaction at this merry time of the year."

"I cannot see what is merry about this time of year at all. The weather is bleak, uncongenial, everything is over-priced, and there is always some violence breaking out at this time, because the poor are even more restless than ever."

"It is from your sister, Mrs. Mayweather."

When hearing that Georgiana had written, Darcy leaned his head against the back of the tub, at Jefferson.

"She has?" he asked.

"Yes. Honestly, I shall always be amazed at how little letters go astray from across the ocean."

"And that's another matter," Darcy sneered. "It's bad enough that she married the wrong man, but to move all the way to New York, to a life she was wholly unaccustomed to."

"Mr. Mayweather is still not favored by the family."

"The entire family did not approve and had every reason to refuse the match. Well, if my sister still wishes to throw herself away, I cannot save her now. In the manner that I did before—"

Darcy cut himself off before he could speak any further on the matter of saving Georgiana from her elopement with Mr. Wickham.

"I'll leave her letter on your desk," Jefferson said.

"That will be unnecessary. I can read and bathe at the same time."

"But if the letter were to drop in the water, sir?"

"When have you known me to be clumsy?"

Jefferson did not attempt to argue but only nodded and left his master alone.

At first, Darcy held the letter in front of him, over the edge of the copper tub.

He stared at Georgiana's name, attached to her husband's last one, from when she had to abandon the title of 'Darcy'. Resentful of the change, he still found the pain of his sister leaving the Darcy-hood and felt her marriage as the betrayal that he took it for.

At last, he opened the letter and read it:

>*Dear Fitzwilliam,*
>*I pray that this letter finds you before the great holiday which makes the bleak midwinter into a time of joy.*

I hope that you are well, and that you have a care to respond to this letter. My last two letters have not been met with any response at all; therefore, I shall merely assume that letters to America have gone astray.

First, I wrote to tell you of a new joy that I shall be fortunate enough to receive.

Once more, you shall be an uncle, for Doctor Donaldson has confirmed that I am with child once more.

Since the first two were a boy and girl, I sincerely hope to be blessed with another little girl that Mr. Mayweather and I can dote on. I think he shall like having another younger version of myself running around. For Christmas presents, I have given my son, Fitz, the traditional presents, and he has shown promise of being a sturdy boy of an open disposition. My daughter is her father's favorite. I am fortunate; parenthood, by its nature, is not the easiest role to undertake, so I confess the fright of being a mother as I also felt the excitement. So, for them to be like their father shows that I have done something right.

Now for the more present matters at hand. I know that you still harbor resentment towards Robert for marrying me, and anxiety towards myself for accepting his offer. I know that you did it out of worry and concern, but I can assure you that Robert still treats me well and loves me.

I have not married a man of vicious or false temperament. His actions were neither mercenary, nor superficial.

When we were engaged, he did not present a false face to lure me in but is the same as he was when we met.

My offer to have you visit us in New York still stands. Colonel Fitzwilliam has already done so and can give proof that I made the correct choice. Put simply, I should like my brother to finally voyage across the Atlantic Ocean and see my family.

I want my children to know their uncle.

When will you forgive me for falling in love?

It would be best for you to come in the summer, because Robert and I are thinking of renting a house in New Jersey, so that you can enjoy your summer by the sea.

Or, if the winter chill is your preference, at least spend Christmas with us.

Please, brother... I know that you have fallen away from man in many respects—but is my brother fully gone? Has he lost all love in him?

If you have not written to me, that shall change nothing. I shall still write to you, in hopes of you replying one day.

Yours etc.

GM

∿

When closing the letter, Darcy let his hand go limp and the paper dropped to the floor.

His sister was a mother again, and she was happy. However, as one does not always turn their minds to what they prefer not to see, Darcy was no exception in the case. Her husband was not the sort of man that he wanted his sister to marry, and despite her letter, he could not believe it. But she was his sister. With his heart being torn with a resolution to never visit her, to another side of himself that wished to do so, Darcy allowed the conflicted aspects of his character to wash over him. Rather than make any decisions on the matter, he would let it lay where it would.

For the moment, he would do nothing. Because, in his

mind, she was another aspect of his life that had abandoned him when he suffered so much abandonment at one time.

And with the harsh reality of his situation, mingled with what he had lost, he fell into a dark place that could not be resurrected and delivered into a happier way.

'Better to do nothing,' Darcy thought to himself. 'For the present, I would do nothing.'

He called Jefferson, informed him that he was done, and Darcy's bath was finished.

At six o'clock, Darcy was dressed for dinner and came down the stairs to eat a solitary meal in his dining room. After he was served, he heard the pit-patter of feet downstairs, indicating that the servants were now leaving to travel to their family's homes for Christmas Eve and Christmas Day.

Mr. Hudson and Mr. Jefferson remained behind to clear away the dinner, complimented their master on giving the servants their wages, and also informed him that maids and footmen were overjoyed at his generosity.

Darcy received all this information with his traditional silence, and went into his parlor, sitting by the fire, taking out a book and reading by the fireplace.

Yet, the flicker of the flames in the hearth danced across the wall and began to—what he thought was—to play tricks on his eyes.

On the wall, opposite him, were two paintings: Darcy's father, and of his mother, Mrs. Anne Darcy.

Despite knowing better, Darcy sensed that there was something irregular about his mother's portrait. After all, paintings do not move. What cannot be denied was that he had perfect vision, so what could it mean that he swore that he saw the portrait shift.

Rather, the figure's face sojourned to not be stationary, but instead—the face moved.

When glimpsing this wondrous and alarming sight, Darcy looked away and dug his body further into his armchair.

He felt a rush of terror wash over him, that comes from viewing a supernatural sight.

Clutching the sides of his chair, Darcy felt a rush of alarm rush along his skin, causing goosebumps to appear.

It could not be!

Yet, despite the terror of seeing a painting come to life, he could not remain there. Feeling curiosity rise up, he looked around his armchair again and looked at the painting.

At first, his mother's portrait was as it was: simply that.

Then came the great change!

The change that the portrait was good upon.

His mother's face suddenly came to life, once more, and slowly, her face turned to see her son.

Darcy remained there, frozen, but his mind was in a state of dread as he saw his mother's image leap to life and stare at him.

It was altogether impossible.

But there his mother was, looking at him through the eyes of artwork. Then she opened her mouth, making her son's eyes widen, as she drove him out of his wits.

'Darcy!' she uttered.

The shock of hearing his mother from a canvas made her son shriek, forcing Darcy backwards as he hit the wall behind him.

The raucous caused Mr. Hudson to rush into the room, worried of any calamity that might have befallen his master. He entered to see Mr. Darcy clutching the wall, his skin practically white with shock, and his face in terror.

"Sir?" Hudson said, "are you well? Has something happened?"

"I saw—"

When looking at the wall again, his mother's portrait gave no indication that there was any paranormal change.

His late mother's portrait was just that, a portrait.

But she was there! She had called his name!

Darcy blinked, and when he opened his eyes again, the portrait was still just that, and he shrugged, considering that it was no more than a trick of the light.

"It's nothing," Darcy said, "my eyes merely were playing tricks on me. But I would prefer a cup of tea."

"As you wish, sir," Mr. Hudson responded, "you look as if you had encountered quite a shock, so tea will help calm your nerves."

Suddenly, there was a knock at the door.

CHAPTER 3

A Man of Good Cheer

"E xcuse me, sir," Mr. Hudson said, and he left Mr. Darcy to answer the door.

"Whoever it is, send them away," Darcy called after him. "I want no visitors tonight!"

Returning to his chair, Darcy picked up his book again, and attempted to read it, but he still felt his mother's eyes on him. Looking around the side of his armchair, he glimpsed the painting again, and still the portrait gave no indication of having a spirit underneath it.

It really was just a moment of failing eyesight, Darcy thought to himself. 'Thank goodness it was a temporary error, and no more. After all, spirits do not exist! Never have and never shall!'.

He was not left in this cloister of isolation for more than a minute before he heard rushed footsteps coming to his parlor door. The knob turned, the door opened, and Darcy only had time to close his book before his cousin, Colonel Richard Fitzwilliam, entered.

"Merry Christmas, Fitz," Colonel Fitzwilliam said, "God save you!"

～

Seeing his cousin enter, with his jovial and animated nature, Darcy had no choice but to lower his book and stand up.

As Colonel Fitzwilliam entered, Mr. Hudson approached behind the Colonel, a little flustered.

"Do not blame your reliable and capable butler," Colonel Fitzwilliam began. "He informed me that you were not receiving visitors, so I decided to come in by forced entry."

"You would," Darcy replied.

"And I *did*." Colonel Fitzwilliam turned to Mr. Hudson, removing his coat, hat, gloves, and handing it to the butler. "How do you do, Hudson?"

"Very well, thank you, Colonel."

"Looking forward to Christmas Day? I pray that you get time to visit your family."

"I have been most fortunate, Colonel," Mr. Hudson replied, "Master Darcy has given me the luxury of having Christmas Day off. Tomorrow morning, I will head for the Borough posthaste. I am looking forward to the day. And I congratulate you on your engagement, sir."

"Thank you, Hudson. I am quite happy."

"I see why. This is the time of the year for joyous events."

"Merry words, sir. Merry words."

"And one must get to the point of your arrival, at some

point," Darcy interrupted, exhausted by the casual conversation that was occurring in front of him.

"Yes, one must, mustn't one?" Colonel Fitzwilliam responded, unwilling to let his cousin's stony attitude affect his merriment.

"I was getting the Master some tea," Hudson responded, "would you be staying for a duration?"

"I could have some tea, but it really depends on how long my cousin can stand my presence, nowadays."

Hudson read in between the lines.

"I shall include another cup," he said, leaving to go to the kitchens.

"Letting off your entire staff for the holidays," Colonel Fitzwilliam said, approaching the fireplace, lifting his jacket tails, so that the fire could warm him faster. "That was kind of you."

"It was against my better judgment," Darcy said, putting his book on his lap.

"Are you looking forward to Christmas yet, or are you still an enemy to the day?" Colonel Fitzwilliam asked.

"Unsupportable!"

"What is unsupportable? My last comment, or Christmas in general?"

"I should think to apply the term to both. Between you and Hudson, what right have you to be merry? He makes no more than twenty shillings a week, and your engagement is questionable, to say the least."

"My engagement is the making of me," Colonel Fitzwilliam said. "In the same way that Georgiana's engagement was also the making of her. But these are absolutes that you do not wish to confront, I presume?"

"And you still say Merry Christmas through this all? What right have you to be merry?"

"It's Christmas; what right have you to be cross?" Colonel Fitzwilliam tapped his head, "oh, now I recall. You are cross because of the mistakes from your past. So, naturally, it must haunt every aspect of your present, and any possibility for congeniality and connection to your fellow man in your future. Fitzwilliam Darcy! The man who ruined his life, and all the wealth in the world cannot save that."

"Are you quite finished, Richard?" Darcy scowled.

"I have not yet begun, I am afraid," Colonel Fitzwilliam retaliated, as light and unaffected as ever.

"If you are looking for a character alteration in me," Darcy responded, "behold! I am what I am, and that will not change."

"Change is the one constant thing in the world, and change is the thing that Richard Fitzwilliam's name is good upon. There is no need to be cross, cousin, but for the grave you dug yourself in."

"I regret nothing," Darcy responded.

"Your nothings are built on *nothing* but suppressed regrets. You may not identify them, but they are there, nevertheless."

"What brings you here, Richard? Other than to seek a victory where you can find none?"

"You know why," Colonel Fitzwilliam responded, as Hudson came in with tea. He prepared it, gave a cup of tea to both cousins, and left as quickly as he had come.

"I have my Christmas party tomorrow," Colonel Fitzwilliam continued, "which is also in celebration of my recent engagement. I am coming to ask you to dine with us. You still have not responded."

"I thought that lack of response was response enough."

"Not for me," Colonel Fitzwilliam said, losing his patience. He leaned forward in the chair he was sitting in, to drive his point even further to conviction. "So, that means that you will not come?"

"I will see you in hell first?"

"Why? Why be so grim, so cold, but for the reason that I have suspected all these years."

Darcy put his cup of tea down, pushed his book on the table sharply, stood up and went to the fireplace. Leaning over for a warmth that would never warm him, Darcy stared into the flames.

"Why do you wish to marry her?" Darcy asked, still looking into the blaze.

"You know why. Because I fell in love with the lady."

Darcy laughed bitterly, and grimaced.

"Because you fell in love!" Darcy felt that he knew the truth, a truth that he felt his cousin overlooked. "There is nothing that I have to say on the matter."

"No, go on," Colonel Fitzwilliam pressed. "I know that you wish to, so I'd much rather hear it."

"Hearing and listening are two different things, and that is the trouble with you." At last, he turned back to his cousin, facing him with his stern gaze. "I can give you all the advice that I can give, yet like Georgiana, you will not listen. Hear, but not listen, and to that, it's proven that wisdom falls on deaf ears."

"What wisdom? All that I hear is that you will not come

to my Christmas dinner on Wimpole Street, because I fell in love with the woman."

"And what should I remember this Christmas for, but a day where you marry a woman who brings no fortune to the match? She marries you for your money, and don't delude yourself on that score."

Colonel Fitzwilliam put down his tea and turned to Darcy sharply.

"Kitty Bennet does no such thing," he retaliated. "You know perfectly well that she loved me before I had the good fortune to receive a vast inheritance. She was willing to marry me before I ever gained my wealth. It was me who spent years putting it off, due to me not having the means to support her. Now I do, and now I can have the love of my life."

"You bring wealth and prestige to a dowerless lady."

"I don't fear the world in that way and never have."

"And when she marries you, what then? What happens when her love proves too expensive? I live in such a world with fools such as this. Merry Christmas, you say? When you find your finances dried, Christmas will no longer be a day to find fondness over but instead turn into a time of paying bills without money, a time for finding yourself a year older and not an hour richer. Christmas will be a time of regret, which you will wish to cover your neck with a branch of holly and hang about the Christmas tree."

"Fitz!"

"Richard! Keep Christmas in your own way and let me keep it in mine."

"Keep it? But you don't keep it."

"Then let me leave it alone."

Straightening his waistcoat, Colonel Fitzwilliam walked over to the window and looked out into the waning light.

"But it can't leave you alone, can it? You mention Christmas as being a time of regret, but you never look toward yourself. All these years, I have explained your taciturn and misanthropic manners because I knew of the disappointments that you have suffered. Even though you brought them onto yourself. But I will not be one to shy from your tones."

With a turning of his countenance, Colonel Fitzwilliam faced his cousin, unafraid, and like that of a soldier.

"The reason that you choose not to dine with us is not because of any wisdom on your part, but out of folly and false pride."

Colonel Fitzwilliam took another step toward his cousin.

"You will not come because of my engagement to Kitty," he continued. "She is perfect for me, and you know this. It was simply our lack of fortune that held us down and gave us both no choice but to fear never catching each other. However, our hearts were always true. Now, I have the wealth to support her, and all is well. So, no. This is not what irks you. No, you will not dine with us because you know that her sister will be there. It's because you don't have the courage to face Elizabeth Bennet again."

When hearing her name, Fitzwilliam Darcy's face blanched, and his expression showed something rare: signs of life. Looking as if he had just been slapped, he buckled momentarily.

Seeing the effect that Elizabeth Bennet's name had on Darcy, Colonel Fitzwilliam decided to pursue the matter, till he reached satisfaction.

"Nonsense," Darcy responded.

"It is not nonsense. You know that Elizabeth Bennet shall be there. And so will Jane Bennet. With the second, when seeing her, you see the woman who you know was perfect for your friend, Charles Bingley, and you separated the two of them forever, damning Bingley to bachelorhood. And with Elizabeth, your loss of viewing her as your wife turned you into a gnarled oak, twisted and ruined forever. The second that you lost her, the second that you lost yourself. No one has the courage to tell you that when you turned your back, on the love of your life, you cursed your own character."

While his cousin said this, Darcy's eyes darkened as he looked at the floor.

"You were once a better man," Colonel Fitzwilliam continued.

Darcy continued looking away.

"You had generosity," he elaborated, "even if it was masked by a proud nature—there was still humanity there. But since you and Elizabeth did not marry, I have watched all of your nobler aspirations die off, one by one, until nothing but an ice-man remains."

Lastly, he walked over to where his tea was, and the Colonel drank the last bit of it.

"Kitty is the love of my life, and I finally found the means to support her. We were practically made for each other. You knew this once. In the same way that Georgiana found a good husband. Yet, because your love, and your life fell apart, then naturally you clutched at every else's happiness like a miser and had to shove everyone's joy into the fire and burn—as yours did. Well, I shall not give into you."

Darcy still didn't respond but only said one thing.

"Good evening."

Seeing that he was not going to be successful, Colonel Fitzwilliam buttoned up his jacket.

"There was a time where you listened to my advice," Colonel Fitzwilliam continued, "and when your heart died, I lost that ability to be an advisor."

"Good evening," Darcy repeated.

"Well, I am sorry to find you so resolute. But my offer still stands. You are always welcome to dine with us, as is the spirit of Christmas."

"Good evening."

"And since I have made the trial in homage to Christmas, I'll keep my Christmas humor to the last. So, Merry Christmas, cousin."

"Good evening."

"And a happy new year."

"Good evening," Darcy responded, slapping his hand against the wall, for emphasis.

Colonel Fitzwilliam walked to the doorway, had another idea, and then turned back to have one last detail to bring forth... for the sake of finding a way to bring about a transformation to the cousin that he once admired.

"There is more to the tale than you know. When Elizabeth finally married, I know that's when another part of you died—even after it was evident that you would not marry her. But still, a part of you never recovered."

Darcy refused to look at his cousin when he unveiled this.

Time had turned Darcy into an indifferent person to this, and he would remain so, until another truth was brought forth.

"Well, I have news to bring you," Colonel Fitzwilliam concluded. "Elizabeth's husband died in the war, in New Zealand. Poor fellow did not pass away easily, from what I have been told. Elizabeth, sweet lady, has been grieving him for the last six months."

"Six months?" Darcy asked, despite having to look curious.

"Yes, Darcy, six months. Never fear, she is still maintaining herself, despite still feeling the loss. And now she is widowed, and single. You have another chance. Take that as you will. And when you are ready to come to Christmas dinner, we shall be happy to see you."

"Good evening," Darcy said, by way of conclusion to the conversation.

"No fear, cousin, for I am done."

Leaving the room, Mr. Hudson showed the Colonel to the door. Both men wished each other a Merry Christmas, and Colonel Fitzwilliam took his leave.

Elizabeth Bennet!

Of course, she was no longer Elizabeth Bennet, but was

Elizabeth Whitaker, to a man who Elizabeth could never see herself happy with—that is, it was so in Darcy's eyes.

But the very concept, the very idea of seeing her again, was enough to rouse Darcy from his inner musings and he gave way to logic. The last thing that he needed to do was to encounter Elizabeth Bennet, and nothing would ever feel the same.

For nothing could.

All Darcy could do was keep her at the safest distance from him, or he was lost.

And then there was Jane Bennet.

Another life that was ruined, according to everyone else who had complained.

Letters of business were all that Darcy required as he sat down at his desk, content to read them and forget about Colonel Fitzwilliam.

Forget about Elizabeth Bennet. Forget about Jane and whom he had separated from a large love of her life. Forget about Georgiana, who left the family to make a new family on the other side of the world.

Darcy ought to have felt that so much came about by the generous spirit of love that was keenly felt at the wonderful time of the year.

But all that he could do was sit down, alone in his parlor, and mutter the word 'nonsense'.

So, Colonel Fitzwilliam, being a man of good cheer, knew that his invitation would still receive no response. Darcy was determined to be cold as ice.

CHAPTER 4

A Spirit Worth the Watching

The night continued, and soon it was Darcy's time to retire. Since he felt that he no longer needed assistance, he allowed Mr. Jefferson to leave him to his own devices.

Although, in truth, it was not done out of the impulse for self-sufficiency, but instead because his spirit was somewhat rattled.

First, he had recalled when he saw flashes of his mother moving from her portrait. This strange vision paled, as he felt, to hearing that Elizabeth Bennet was still out in the world. This, he knew, of course, but to be out in the world, and unattached.

As quickly as he considered the matter, he dismissed it, only for it to still return to the forefront of his mind. He could not release thinking of her, despite his desire to do the reverse. The best remedy that Darcy could concoct was sleep. A good night of rest could refresh him, and he would wake up with renewed vigor, and a grander sense of mind.

Elizabeth Bennet and he had parted ways for years, and

the next day, he would realize the wisdom of that choice, on both their parts.

With candle in hand, Darcy moved through the darkness, ascending the stairs to his bedroom. Usually, being such a solitary fellow, Darcy did not fear the dark. Yet, with the servants gone, he could not deny being sensitive that, excepting his manservant, he was quite alone.

The dark was, for once, not his friend, nor his constant companion that gave him the excuse to remain at home and to himself, where he was often content to be quiet and comfortable.

And then he recalled the way Elizabeth Bennet would laugh. Recalling that sound made him stop midway, and he remained motionless on the step.

Closing his eyes, Elizabeth's image surfaced in his thoughts, and her laughter—which he once declared as the sweetest sound he would ever hear—had filled the emptiness of his house. When he opened his eyes again, he recalled that he was quite alone and was ashamed of his own foolishness.

"Unsupportable," he muttered. After all, nothing was more useless, in his opinion, than regret.

In his bedroom, Jefferson had everything prepared.

His dressing gown was already hanging up, and there was a fire in the fireplace, with a candle on his nightstand, and a book next to it. Jefferson was aware that his master enjoyed reading in bed.

He closed the door behind him, put down his candle on a table, went over to his mirror, and looked at himself as he began to remove his jacket. As he began to unbutton his waistcoat, the fire suddenly erupted very passionately.

"What the devil?" Darcy asked, approaching it, and beginning to move the logs around, with a hot poker, to make it blaze correctly.

Once he got it in order, he heard the clock bells strike the hour.

Only it was not the hour.

Not the hour at all.

Darcy looked at the clock in his room and saw that it was merely 10:15.

Then the clock bells began to sound in another room.

"What the devil is going on?"

Inwardly, he was disturbed but also fascinated.

The bells did not end after the finish of the minute, but suddenly, the bells began to sound all throughout the house.

Even Big Ben had something to say of the matter. Big Ben clock, standing atop that magnificent building, the Elizabeth Tower, in the heart of London, rang its five bells, that seemed to reach out all the way from the Westminster District, and Darcy felt it keenly, that he had no choice but to hold his ears as he crouched down, overwhelmed by the sound.

It was as if every bell in London had extended its power, found its way to Berkley Square, and descended upon him.

"Stop!" Darcy cried. "What is happening?"

At the utterance of his plea for it to end, the bells ceased, and the sound progressed from mayhem to silence.

Darcy removed his hands from his ears and looked around.

The pain was over.

Yet the confusion was still there.

"Jefferson?" Darcy whispered, surprised that his manservant had not come to see him, equally as perplexed as he was by what happened. "Where is he?"

Darcy was met with no answer, until the response was a melody.

Downstairs, he heard music. Someone was playing the pianoforte, an instrument that no longer was of use, but was there for display.

After all, the only one who played it was Georgiana— and his mother. Aware that it could be neither one of them, Darcy froze.

The musical tune was familiar to him, yes, because he had heard it before. Yet, there was something ominous about the music, even though the melody was light and uplifting.

After all, Darcy was wholly aware that neither Jefferson, nor Hudson, knew how to play.

So, who could it be?

At first, Darcy remained there, crouched on the floor, unwilling to move. From seeing his mother move in the painting. From hearing the bells filling his house. Now, to music playing from someone who ought not to be there.

To nothing being right!

The terror!

The alarm!

Anyone else would buckle and cower in the same fashion. Ergo, Darcy's reaction was natural, and it would root him to the spot. But nothing could be achieved by remaining where he was. Therefore, Darcy gathered his courage, stood up, and walked slowly to the door.

Filled with trepidation, he turned the knob and opened it with such a slow speed that it took a whole minute. Once the door was ajar by a few inches, he poked his head out, looking along the landing, and he saw through the dark, somewhat.

There was no one there, and no one on the large and majestic staircase. Yet the music still washed over him.

Darcy was not a fool, however, and was aware of the dangers of walking downstairs, defenseless. Quickly, he walked back to his fireplace, took the poker, prepared to use it like that of a sword, and exited his room again.

"Jefferson?" Darcy whispered, but still there was no one. "What trick is this?"

Slowly, he approached the staircase, and tiptoed gently down one step, and then the other. Without a doubt, the piano was being played in the parlor.

Careful and calculating, Darcy moved along the wall, reached the doorway to the parlor, then he leaned in, looking in to see a figure playing on the magnificent instrument.

It was the back of a woman, with her hair done up, wearing an elegant gown, and she was a master as she flew her hands over the piano keys.

At first, Darcy was alarmed. And yet, when seeing the figure of a lady, his fears calmed down, and it was replaced merely by astonishment.

Especially when he sensed, rather than knew, that there was something less-than-natural about this elegant lady who was playing in his parlor. He could not put words to it, and he did not need to.

It was still, despite it all, a conundrum, that Darcy should be more alarmed by. In truth, he was a little terrified, because he didn't know what to make of what was before him.

However, he was also intrigued. And the woman who played! What of her?

First, she was drained of all color. Her image and outline were blacker and whiter than anything else. It was as if he was watching a figure drawn on the page with pens now come to life. Also, her hair and dress swayed in the air, as if there was a perpetual wind that brushed along her, where it did not to the rest of the room. Lastly, her manner of dress was very odd, because of it no longer being fashionable. She was dressed in the fashions that were popular during regency times almost twenty years ago.

Looking closely at the woman's hands, Darcy found himself falling into the rhythm of the music that she was playing, and it began to fill his heart and mind.

For a brief moment, Darcy let the music wash over him and put him at ease. Until the terror of the moment reinserted itself and Darcy returned to fearing the figure.

At the end of the piece, the woman stopped playing and remained sitting on the piano bench.

"Fear," the woman said, who's figure was floating on the invisible winds, "I can see into your heart. You don't wish to learn of me, or who I was."

"Who are you?" Darcy asked, his voice breathy. "Who *were* you?"

"In life, I was your mother," the specter said, turning to face him. "Anne Darcy."

His mother!

Now that she had turned, he gathered a full view of the shade's face. His eyes widened as he saw the form, figure, and face of the woman who raised him. The woman who loved him. The woman who was always there for him... until the last bit of her light had gone out.

And yet, Darcy was a man of logic. As a result, it was only natural to assume that he was not seeing anything remotely true and real. After all, his mother could not possibly be there. For nothing about this could belong to the realm of reality.

Yet, there his mother was, sitting at her piano, as she had always done so. And she did so again, just as natural as ever.

The chief difference was that her figure still lacked all color, was drenched in the whites, grays and blacks that is often used to describe an apparition.

"Won't you sit down?" Anne Darcy asked her son.

Darcy still did not move.

His mother cocked her head to the side, reading her son's expression, and sensing his inability to accept the supernatural element that was her. That was everything he was now experiencing.

"You do not believe, do you?" Anne asked. "You do not believe in me, or that I am truly here."

"No," Darcy said, his voice still hoarse from disbelief. "No, I do not."

"But I am here."

"You are not. My mother is gone," Darcy said, with an ache in his voice that indicated emotion. He was beginning to feel the pain of when he lost her before, and it betrayed him.

"I cannot believe," Darcy continued, his voice losing its strength even more and more, being reduced to a whisper. "You are not here."

"Although you do see me," Anne Darcy responded, "why do you doubt your senses? Blindness never became you when I was alive, but it does now. Stronger than ever."

"Because a little thing affects them. Illness, delusions, and dreams. For all that I know, I could easily not be here but fallen into the recesses of my mind and dreamed something that is not real. My mother is gone, so there is more fantastical than fact about you, whatever you are."

Anne Darcy suddenly stood up, her figure sharp, her position defined, as she roared out.

"Enough!" she cried.

Her declaration was loud, like that of thunder, and as if the heavens had cracked open and pushed its will upon the world.

This forced her son to be knocked against the wall, cowering like a little boy being chastised.

"Enough!" she cried again, raising out her arms. "Son, look upon me!"

A wind swept through the fireplace, and Darcy noticed that from around the hem of his mother's gown, he saw many papers, with writing on it, swiveling around her feet and then they rose up and rushed toward Darcy. The papers were so large in number that they began to fill the floor, and crawled around the wood, like they were living and breathing things.

Darcy's eyes widened as he felt chastised under his mother's gaze, and the force of the wind had pushed him to the floor, clutching his body to fend away the air.

The papers that had continued to exude from his mother rushed at him, rolling themselves over and under his person, covering his entire person, and sometimes falling on his face.

He was blinded by one sheet of paper that had covered his face, and he was ignorant of what was around him.

When he gathered the strength to move the paper from his face, he only had time to read the words 'Dear sister Catherine…' before the wind knocked the paper from out of his hand and flew up in the air.

He looked at his mother before she raised out her arm, clearly controlling all the sheets on the floor.

The papers obeyed, rising up in the air, and filling the scene like they were raindrops pouring down.

Son of mine, Anne Darcy's voice said in her son's mind. Her mouth was closed, but he heard the words easily. *Do you believe in me, or not?*

I do, Darcy uttered, from his thoughts, but not out loud. *I do.*

Anne Darcy snapped her fingers, the wind stopped, and the papers disappeared. When the wind slowed down, Darcy felt that he controlled his limbs again, rose to his knees, and stood up.

"You really are my mother?" Darcy asked.

"I am, Fitzwilliam. Believe in me as you believe in your senses. I am your mother."

Forgetting his stoic nature and sardonic inclinations, only then did it occur to him that he regained the mother that he had lost.

"I should not believe it."

"But you do because I am real. Not a trick of the mind, but true. Son!"

"Mother!"

Darcy rushed to her as she extended her arms, to embrace him.

Repeating this action, Darcy was prepared to wrap his arms around her, but he rushed through the specter and felt a coldness as if he had braved passing through a cold wind.

When he opened his eyes, he didn't see his mother in his arms, but she was behind him, with her arms pressed against her body, where she had attempted to hug him, and was unable to.

Turning to her, Darcy felt embarrassed, and his mother felt powerless.

"I would embrace you," Anne Darcy said, emotionally and maternally, "more than anything, I would wish to hold my child again."

Slowly, she approached him, raised up her arm and rested her hand as close to her son's face, without swiping through it.

"Yet, this is the closest that I can achieve."

"I cannot even hold you," Darcy whispered, overcome.

"I am sorry," Anne replied, lowering her hand from his face, "so much it hurts me, as it does you."

"You died too soon," Darcy choked.

"No true mother ever wants to leave her child. All life ends, even when we want to stay by your side."

"Why did you not come before?" Darcy hissed. "You did not come to see me sooner!"

"It takes a while to return to this world in this manner," his mother assured him. "And the spirit is energy. When death arrives, it gets changed, and becomes like that of gust of a wind, blowing about, and wandering far and wide. For death is a part of life, and all things must end so that something else can begin. It was right for me to remain away, so that you could live, look for your happiness, and love as was your right."

"I have done my duty," Darcy stated. "I have done right."

"My boy," his mother said, sadness filling her eyes, "I love you, but you have not. I come back from the other side of the veil to make amends for the wrongs that I have committed."

"What wrongs?" Darcy asked.

Anne Darcy looked at him squarely in the face, bearing her intentions in his eyes.

"I am looking upon it."

Darcy flinched.

"I have done everything that is proper and correct," Darcy said.

"Again, I love you, but you have not."

Darcy's eyes flickered with disappointment. His mother was returned to him and the first thing that she spoke of was that he had failed to live up to her expectations.

"What do you want with me?" Darcy asked.

"Much," his mother replied, and her eyes narrowed on

his. "Much indeed. When life left me, I never stopped caring for you and Georgiana. But my woes now have nothing to do with her because she has found her way. With you, my boy, my heart, I never knew what I was doing. I never knew where I was leading you."

Darcy stood up, walked across the room, and folded his arms as he stared over the fireplace.

"You are angry with me," his mother replied, "whenever you lean against the fireplace like that, it always showed your anger."

"You disappoint me, mother."

"Do I? Why?"

"Because here you are, come to me once more, and all you talk of is me not living up to your expectations. What expectations have not been met?" Darcy wheeled back on her. "I have maintained our family's wealth, intended to marry Anne de Bourgh, and kept the Darcy name respectable, keep Pemberley prosperous and have sacrificed any other way of living for the sake of keeping the name Darcy immortal. All I have done was by your instructions and teachings. And you chastise me for doing my duty."

"Duty!" Anne Darcy scoffed. "Your heart was my duty! All the principles that I taught you, charity, benevolence, love of your fellow man and woman was my duty. And above all, to have happiness in your life was choosing your path. And that included the woman who you really loved. My legacy frightened you from making that choice, and I have spent many years watching you from above, below, and beyond, dying day by day, because of the choices that you did not make."

His mother sat down on the piano stool.

"And I can bear it no longer. I had to return to you, because, between the two of us, I am not the one who is lifeless. Never believe that I do not love you now. I come for your soul and shall give you what I ought to have given. My stay on this earth is brief, Fitzwilliam. And my time is nearly gone. Please, look upon your mother now."

Giving in, Darcy turned back. After all, how could he refuse, especially since he was now informed that his time with his mother was brief. When doing so, he noticed all the papers on the floor that still revolved around her feet.

"You are trailed with paper and words," he noted. "Why?"

"All of these are letters to your aunt, Lady Catherine de Bourgh. To my sister, filled with our intentions on how we could dictate and order our children's lives. From the very beginning, we had a dream, and it was beautiful to us. Letters upon letters, words on words, and paper filled with a goal that we pressed upon you and my niece.

"We took away the chief choice that you both had the right to make, destroying the path that was the natural road for you both to walk down. You and Anne de Bourgh were not in love and never were. Neither of you would have made the other happy, but we were blind. My sister and I were mistaken and meant well. And now, she and I are fettered down by the many dreams that we choked our children with. I made this trail of letters that hold me down as I walk about. I made it, word by word, page by page, and within every letter, each cry out 'regret'. Regret!"

His mother looked at her son, with such concern and love, that Darcy felt it, despite his bitterness.

"And my actions led to you losing love, losing what

could have given you the spark you needed to kindle your heart. Now, there is no warmth to build the foundations of your soul. My son has grown cold to himself, to the thoughts and feelings of others, to his own family, and thus to the world."

She picked up one of the letters that trailed her person and held it in front of him.

"The weight of this train holds me down to such an extent that I live hard by it. Do you know the length and weight of your own train, Fitzwilliam? Since I have died, you have labored upon it. It is a ponderous train."

"Mother, what do you want of me?" Darcy asked. "Behold. This is who I am."

"No," his mother argued, "this is who you are, but not what you are meant to be. Your heart is your duty. Your heart is your business. And you shall ignore it, no longer!"

Throwing the page she held in the fire, the flames erupted into a fierce blaze as it consumed the paper. Suddenly the bells began to sound all throughout the house.

Bells ringing—not only from within, but also from without.

From every church in London, to Big Ben, signaling the hour of discontent, 'change' rang.

Once more, Darcy covered his ears, moving back and forth to survive the deafening noise. Being a shade, his mother was not affected by the sound, physically. Yet, being a ghost from the other side, she was affected by the sound, emotionally.

While her son tried to protect himself, her eyes were wistful, as she moved to the window and looked out, in the winter night.

"I can stay only for one more minute. The time of my departure is now wrung."

The bells died down immediately, and Fitzwilliam turned to his mother's specter.

"Already!" Darcy cried. "You cannot leave me now." He dashed toward her. "I will not have it. I will not have you go."

Once more, he rushed into her and therefore rushed through her.

Sadly, they turned back to each other.

"I never left you," she assured him, desperate. "And by taking this course of action, I show you that I never will leave you. I have come to warn you and do everything that I can to save you from suffering my fate. I am come to give you a better way."

"You still love me."

"Always. Never did I turn my back upon your fate. I am the beginning, and the end, but not the middle. In that time, you shall be haunted by three spirits."

When hearing that, Darcy was apprehensive and discomforted.

"I will be haunted?"

"Yes."

"Mother, I do not want that."

"I am your mother, so you shall have it. Each one shall take you on a path that will lend much reflection and reckonings. Without these visits, you cannot hope to escape the path that you are now set upon. I bring you hope, and I will believe in you finding it."

Once more, she attempted to place her hand on her son's cheek. Filled with childlike affection, Darcy tried to cover her hand with his, to the best of his ability.

He lost his mother, and now he sensed that he would lose her again.

"Must you go?" he whispered.

"I must, for you to come to a better way. Look to the visits, which will be signaled by the music that finds you. And heed their words."

Suddenly, the window to the parlor opened and the coldness of the night pushed through, bringing winter into the parlor.

"Look out as I depart," she said, going to the piano, and playing a beautiful piece of music, "and see the trains of regret. You will find it when you listen to the music of the night."

As she began to play, her figure lost its form, turned into a shapeless aura of light, that rose in the air, was ejected from the window, and escaped into the night.

Between curiosity, compassion and hearing the music that never left the air, Darcy rushed to the window to see where his mother's spirit had gone.

When he did, she was no longer there.

However, the music continued. It was a beautiful and bittersweet tune that suddenly turned eerie, as well as a little haunting.

Turning to where the music rose higher, he saw figures along the street. Like his mother, these figures were not corporeal or living. Rather, they were ghosts of people in the past.

As they walked, between passersby on the street, a trail of papers followed them, like the train his mother had.

With some, the train was shorter.

With others, it was longer.

At first, it swiveled around them, weighing them down, making them walk slower than they could have.

Suddenly, they all stopped.

Darcy's eyes widened as he witnessed over a hundred shades stop where they were, closed their eyes, and suddenly, all the letters, the papers written by themselves, of choices that ought not to have been made that held them down, that kept them from living the life that they ought to have—began to rise.

It was as if it was a moment of acknowledgement, or prayer, was occurring. That they came together, as one, to recognize the error they committed from when they lived.

All those papers rose up in the air, as spirit-like as the persons who wrote them and filled the night sky.

The spectacle did not end on that street, however, as Darcy stretched his focus, far beyond Berkley Square, he saw papers rising in every street as far as he could see.

The ghosts filled every road in London.

How many people who repented their actions, to the point where they could not rest, could not be given the peace that death was meant to give them.

No! They lived in torment. And his mother went through this? Did his father?

How many men and women, who had come before

him, who had pages trailing after them so, rather than resting in their grave.

In an instant, as is the way with human nature, we can look upon a large spectacle, a grand scene, and then narrow our focus to one image.

This was what Darcy had encountered.

One of the shades on Berkley Square had looked away from where his pages and words were gliding. Turning his head, he focused on Darcy.

The music became more haunting.

Unlike all the other ghosts, this was the only one that noticed the Master of Pemberley.

Their eyes locked gazes.

In the ghost's eyes was wonder.

In Darcy's eyes was bewilderment.

After a few seconds, where the music of the night had reached a chilling pitch, the ghost opened his mouth and roared at Darcy.

The roar was one word, to stress his pain, which was the same pain that all the specters felt.

That Anne Darcy felt.

"Regret!"

The word, and the manner which it was shouted was so frightening that it led to Darcy gasp. He quickly shut the window and closed the curtain.

When doing so, Darcy moved away from that side of the parlor, rushed to the armchair that was near the fire and slumped in it.

What is going to happen? he asked himself. "What is going to happen?"

CHAPTER 5

The First of Three Spirits

After experiencing such a shock, sleep should not find a person that easily. Yet with Darcy, there was no choice but to be exhausted by what he had witnessed. Or perhaps, it was what was meant to happen when witnessing so many apparitions, that it made the soul and mind weary.

Refusing to go to bed, he sat down in the parlor, afraid to move. Instead, he only remained in the armchair by the fire, letting the warm flames serve as his companion.

Hudson and Jefferson could not help him, because this all seemed as if they were ignorant of what was occurring. It must have been purposeful.

Darcy had the inclination to defy his mother's advice, and wake his manservant and butler, but the exhaustion did magically take hold of him, and sleep became like a blanket, folding over the man, as he felt his eyelids grow heavy.

Instinctively, he kept trying to keep his eyes open, but it was useless. Even with all he witnessed, an unknown force brought on the word 'sleep', and Darcy was ignorant that he had drifted off. Yet, drifted off, he did.

His sleep was deep, but it was not to be long lasting. For after a couple of hours, he was forced out of his dreams—or nightmares—by the sound of music.

Opening his eyes, he jerked forward, and his gaze was met by a darkened room.

The fire had gone out, and since it was natural to call for assistance, Darcy spoke before thinking.

"Hudson, the fire is out!" He got no response. "Jefferson?"

"They cannot hear you," came a voice from the pianoforte in the corner.

The response was followed by music coming from the piano.

Leaning his head around the side of the chair, slowly, he looked at the strange voice who said it.

He had a reason to be frightened, for while there was music, there was no one playing it.

There was a voice—but no one was there to utter it.

Suddenly a fire materialized in the fireplace, illuminating the room.

"What is a blind man that cannot see?" the voice said, but Darcy still saw no one.

"I am not blind," Darcy replied, his voice shaky from fear. After all, when hearing a voice, but seeing no image, can be terrifying to the strongest of individuals. Even Darcy was not fully stone. "I cannot see what is not there."

"Because you have not taken the time to come forward

and acknowledge me at first. Come to my voice and open me."

At first, Darcy was hesitant.

"And do not call for your manservants," the voice said. "Neither of them can assist you now. Do not fear the melody."

"I fear nothing," Darcy said, standing up. He gathered his courage and walked toward the piano.

Still no one was there.

The piano played, with no one stroking the keys. However, there was a slight illumination coming from an object that was on the desk. It was a book that he had never seen before, or yet heard of:

The Chimes of Midnight

The book had a warm, but unnatural glow that left Darcy both unnerved as well as enthralled. He froze; he also could not look away.

"Open me, and see the knowledge that I give," the book cried.

Darcy remained frozen, still unable to believe what was unfolding all around him.

"The longer that you refuse my existence," the voice said, "the longer you defer what you must endure, nevertheless. Come, Darcy, and learn of me."

Closing his eyes, Darcy breathed out and in. When he opened his eyes, he found his courage again, reached out and placed his hand on the book. When feeling it, he felt as if there a strange sort of transference, as if a bit of his energy had been drained from him but was rewarded by the light that the book gave off in turn.

Slowly, he opened the front of the book and then flipped the pages.

After a couple of seconds, the book lit up and began to shake.

Backing away from the disturbed volume, Darcy saw the light begin to grow more and more pronounced so that he had to shield his eyes.

As he squinted, he saw a hand emerging from the book, then another hand, an arm, a head, a torso, a waist, legs, and feet. From the small dimensions of the story, a whole woman had emerged as she materialized, sat down at the pianoforte and began to play.

"Does the light hurt your eyes?" she asked, as she ran her hands gracefully over the piano keys.

"Yes," Darcy said, "please diminish it enough for me to see you!"

"Very well," she said, nodding to the book—a book that closed on its own. When it did, the light lowered enough for the spirit to be seen.

After such, Darcy was now able to look directly at the shade who emerged from the words of a story.

Now he saw her, and could mark what he marked, and ascertained what he ascertained.

The woman was young, handsome in her own way, and her clothes were out of fashion. Rather than it being the proper fashion of the day, this woman was wearing an attire that belonged more to an earlier time in England, from the beginning of the 19th century. Her hair was done up in a classical style, and her dress was more comfortable and of a high waistline, with flat boots that marked a freer time for the lady.

He once recalled that his mother dressed like that.

For a moment, Darcy was lost in the memory of that, before he became aware of what he was being coerced into.

"You still do not believe in me either," the woman said, while still playing. "Do you?"

Darcy moved away from the woman, paced to the other side of the room, placed his arms behind his back and looked out the window.

"I still am afraid to, but you are here, nevertheless," Darcy responded. "You are the spirit who's coming was foretold to me?"

"Indeed, I am," the apparition said, while still playing on.

"Who are you?" Darcy asked. "I must ask, despite not being introduced first."

"I am not a lady who must stand on ceremony, even if I look like it. As such, loss of etiquette does not wound me."

"I suppose it would not be, for a ghost."

The woman smiled and continued to play.

"Thus, I do not have to stand on ceremony," Darcy stated, "and how glad I am of it. Who, or what are you?"

The woman did not look at Darcy, but at the book that she emerged from.

"I have gone by many names," she began, "but that is not who I am now. My image is here, but my aura goes further back to many days before. I am the Ghost of Christmas Past."

The ghost had been reading from sheet music but did

not require anyone to turn the page. Rather, the pages turned on their own.

"Past?" Darcy repeated. "Who's past? Humanity's past? An animal's past? Britain's past? My family's past? You must be precise, or I shall be left in the dark."

"You are very precise, for a human."

"I prefer clarity. Even from a spirit. Is the past a past from long ago?"

"No. It is *your* past."

My past, Darcy thought. 'What could be special for my past to be brought forth?'

"Much," the ghost answered his question, "much can be special from recalling your many days gone by and you left them behind."

"A man ought not to dwell on the past."

"A man also should not ignore the past, or they would be doomed to repeat it," the spirit retorted. "I come for your welfare, whether your witty words will attempt to withstand my mission—that is of your own affair. No matter what, you shall come with me."

"I do not wish to go," Darcy said, straightening his waistcoat and heading for the door, "this business is concluded."

The music stopped abruptly as the door closed in his face. Immediately, Darcy attempted to open it, but he was locked in.

"Have a care, man," Christmas Past said, "the more you refuse, the more you make the matter difficult."

"I do not see how going with you can be conducive to my welfare."

"Then I speak for your reformation, then. And your redemption."

"I like the man that I am."

"But is it the man that you felt you ought to have been?"

Darcy opened his mouth and then closed it.

As Christmas Past stood up, she gestured to the book, it floated in the air and flew into her hands. When observing the novel, Darcy felt some sort of illumination coming from within.

"Why do you carry it with you?" he asked. "Do you live in the narrative?"

"We're all a part of a story, somehow," she said, gesturing to 'The Chimes of Midnight' that she now had levitating in the air. "This book is filled with humanity's *regrets*. Every person that I have met in my travels has had those. Yet some have regrets, so large in number, weight, and magnitude, that it found its way into this book, to the point where the story is limitless. I shall show your past, with an attempt to find yourself in the pages of this volume. You shall walk with me."

"Where shall we walk?"

"Into many days long past—and all of them connected to yours. When hearing the music, you have heard the chimes of midnight, and what it predetermines. It's the time of a new day."

It would have been in vain for Darcy to plead that he was ill-suited to go walking about to a place he still doubted could happen. Especially since the weather and the hour were not adapted to pedestrian purposes.

As he considered that he ought to bring up these impediments, Past raised up the book, let it float into the middle of the room and it rested gently on the floor.

When it did so, the book opened, flipped to the middle chapter, and a light began to shine from it.

Once more, the music began to play, as the light pushed back all the walls and furniture in the room.

"What is happening?" Darcy cried.

"The chimes of midnight, man," Past said. "The chimes of midnight."

Darcy was left to move to the left and right, frontwards and backwards, as the room moved away, giving space for a larger scene to slide in.

His chairs and sofa were moved backward, the pianoforte was slid out, the fire screen rose up and disappeared into an invisible atmosphere.

The whirlwind of his home dissolving and a new scene entering made Mr. Darcy become off-kilter.

When the scene fell into place, he was standing in a field of snow on the edge of a large estate that he was all too familiar with.

He was not alone, however. The spirit was standing next to him, with her book hovering next to her, like a trusty companion that loyally remained at her side.

Before them was a large, impressive, and imposing house that augmented the grandiosity of the woman who ran it.

"You know this place," Past said, standing at Darcy's side.

"Know it! Of course, I do. This is the home of my aunt, Lady Catherine de Bourgh. It is Rosings Park."

Darcy and Christmas Past remained standing along the snow, as Darcy looked around and marked a difference to how things must be in the present day.

"But that is not right," Darcy said, gesturing to a tree. "I could have sworn that tree was larger. And there was a fence, over yonder? It's all wrong because the entire garden is altered."

"Not altered," the spirit said, "but younger than as you know it. You are not looking at the Rosings Park of today, but as it was when you were children. This is the day when your family came down from the North, for Christmas."

As if she had summoned it, a chaise and four came down the lane, followed by another carriage that bore luggage and the servants who attended the family.

The two vehicles arrived at the front door, and servants exited from Rosings Park, eager to meet the new arrivals.

The first carriage doors opened, and a respectable-looking man in his late thirties stepped down from the carriage to offer his hand to the other women who he traveled with.

"Father!" Darcy uttered, going forward, and losing all his harsh habits. When seeing his father again, his face lit up, and he took some quick steps forward. Next, his mother stepped down, and his heart was even warmer, because it was when she was in the very flowers of motherhood, alive and as he remembered her.

As was natural, he raised his arm to wave to them both.

"Mother and Father!" he cried. "It's me? It's Fitzwilliam."

"These are but shadows of the things that have been," Past explained, "they can neither see, nor hear you."

"But I can see them," Darcy said, his voice gentle and overcome. "To see them again."

After Anne Darcy was handed down from the chaise, she looked back into it.

"Come out, little Fitzy," she said, reaching in and pulling a child out of it.

Darcy's eyes widened as he saw his six-year-old self leaping into his mother's arms as she carried him out, where the servants ushered them in.

"That's me," Darcy whispered, "but as a boy. So small, was I not?"

"At that age, what child is not?" Past asked. "As, with that age, what child is not innocent, not destroyed by the pains that life puts on us as we grow?"

"When we age, we have responsibilities," Darcy augmented. "They change everything."

"What is the point of being grown, if the child inside of you wholly dies?"

Darcy did not respond but remained looking at his family as they were ushered into Rosings Park, while the servants took all their things into the house.

"They have gone inside," Darcy said, "we cannot see them, despite that I remember this Christmas."

"But we can," Past said as she raised the book in front of them. The light that emitted from 'The Chimes of

Midnight' enveloped them, their figures fell into the book, and Darcy felt as if he had fallen through oblivion.

At last, the light faded, and he and the spirit were hurled out of the book and appeared into an inner chamber room, where an imposing woman entered. Her tone, look, and figure was regal and stately, even though her face had no applications of being lovely. She was hand-some, however, to be sure. In her face was the youth that Darcy's mother possessed, since she was a great deal younger.

"You both did not arrive within the hour that you said that you would," she declared, kissing Darcy's mother on the cheek. "I warned you about traveling around this time of day."

"Nonsense, sister," Anne Darcy said, "we have made good time."

"That's your aunt, is it not?" Christmas inquired.

"Yes, when she still lived," Darcy said, equally amazed. "My aunt, Lady Catherine de Bourgh."

"And here is your handsome nephew," Anne Darcy said, taking Young Darcy by the hand. "Fitzy, say Merry Christmas to your Aunt Catherine."

Darcy, at the tender age of six, stepped forward and said Merry Christmas pleasantly to his aunt.

"Good," Lady Catherine responded. "It is best for you to learn perfect manners at your age, nephew, for one day, you shall run a large empire of land, and I cannot afford for you to be anything less than proper."

Being a child, the young Darcy only could focus on his aunt when she said this.

Yet, now, with Darcy standing by next to Past, and

watched the scene from another point of view, Darcy saw how his father rolled his eyes at this comment.

"Oh, for god sakes, Catherine," Mr. Darcy Sr. declared, "it is Christmas. None of that."

"It is never too early, and I will not be argued with."

Lady Catherine bent down.

"Now, Nephew," Lady Catherine said, "you must do right by me again, and kiss your aunt on the cheek."

The Young Darcy looked up at his mother, nervous. She nodded to her son, who accepted that he had no choice in the matter.

Stepping forward, with his knees shaking, Young Darcy approached his aunt and kissed her on the cheek.

"Good," Lady Catherine said, "family is the most important thing, little nephew, especially during Christmastime."

"Yes, Aunt," Young Darcy responded, meekly.

"In truth," Mr. Darcy said as he stood next to Christmas Past, going unnoticed by everyone, "I feared my Aunt Catherine. When you are a child, you understand, she creates a shadow over you, that is larger than life."

"You did?"

"Yes."

"Do you still fear her?" Past asked. This led to Darcy scoffing at such a preposterous thing to inquire about.

"What is there to fear? My Aunt passed away three years ago. Now that she is gone, there is no reason to feel alarm."

"Does the shadow of her memory still haunt you, though, even to this very day?"

Darcy groaned. "Do not mock me, shade."

Suddenly, a woman entered, with a little girl trailing behind her.

"That is Mrs. Jenkinson," the Older Darcy said to Christmas Past. "She was widowed at a young age and had been an old school friend to my aunt. She was actually a very nice woman but was not blessed with any child. I never felt any fear when I was in her presence. When her husband died, my aunt took her into her service, and she became my cousin's personal servant. It was all well, because Mrs. Jenkinson always wanted to have children, so looking after my cousin was as good a fortune as any."

The woman, Mrs. Jenkinson, was beautifully plump and had a robust look to her, which was a stark contrast to the little girl who she tended to.

Being a child, the little girl was naturally small. However, the color of her complexion was always somewhat pale. The child was stricken with a sickly constitution, which naturally left the poor child miserable. Mix her poor state of health with an overpowering mother who oversaw an estate and had to appear as strong at all times, and life may have been comfortable, but it didn't signify that it was easy.

"Mrs. Jenkinson," Lady Catherine said, "there you are. Sister, brother, and nephew, you shall see how well my little Anne is doing."

The child was her daughter, Anne de Bourgh.

Anne de Bourgh was presented to the family.

"There is my little namesake," Mrs. Darcy said,

approaching her niece, and kissing her on the cheek. "How does our little Anne do?"

Anne de Bourgh did not respond, but it was not entirely her fault. In truth, Anne was wholly ignorant of what she wanted to say, for what child, at six years old, always knows what to say?

Even so, once Anne tried to speak, she began to cough a little.

"Mrs. Jenkinson, Anne needs to return to the nursery and take her medicine," Lady Catherine said.

"Oh, but it is just a little bit of a cough," Mrs. Jenkinson objected gently. "This was Anne's chance to see her family, and she was looking forward to it. Weren't you, Anne?"

Anne smiled gently at her but did not respond.

"You are wrong. Take her back to the nursery."

Mrs. Jenkinson had no choice but to give in, and Anne was taken away once more.

"She will be better prepared when it is time for dinner."

"I remember this moment," Darcy whispered, moving passed the spirit and up to his younger self. "This was the beginning of my duty being pressed upon me. You shall see, spirit, you shall see."

"I suppose that I shall," Past responded.

Lady Catherine looked at the boy Darcy, and a scheme was afoot.

"And what better way to make my little Anne feel better than to have her cousin go upstairs and entertain her. He should go upstairs to the nursery and keep his cousin company."

"But she might not want me to," the boy Darcy blurted out, excitedly.

"And I was correct," Darcy said to the spirit, "she did not want me there."

"Nonsense," Lady Catherine said, "and as a child, you will not contradict me at all."

"Sister, he did not mean to offend, I assure you," Mrs. Darcy said, "that is all. Perhaps he did it for Anne's sake. After all, if she is ill, my little Fitzy was worried about disturbing her."

"Poppycock," Lady Catherine dismissed. "They are both of the same age, and what better way to help their bond grow than to know that Anne will always have Fitz by her side when she is ill." Lady Catherine focused all her attention on her young nephew. "After all, their bond is already naturally strong. Isn't it, my nephew?"

Young Darcy did not respond to this question, because he was learning more and more, that Aunt Catherine did not require a response to anything.

"Even at that age?" Christmas Past brought up.

"Yes," Darcy said, looking down at his younger self, and pitying him. "Even at so young an age, the concept of duty was pressed on me. And I learned it well."

"Perhaps a little too well, in this circumstance," Christmas Past said.

"It was what my mother and aunt wanted," Darcy said. "I so much wanted to make them happy and honor their memory."

Young Darcy was ushered out of the room and taken to the nursery to keep Anne de Bourgh company.

"When I got up there, it was a dreary and dismal

thing," Darcy explained to the spirit. "Mrs. Jenkinson did not understand why it was pressed on me to play vigil to my cousin, and Anne did not want to even talk to me. I spent half an hour in the corner, doing nothing, until Jenkinson brought some games into the room and played them with me. I asked Anne if she wanted to play, but she was happy to remain in bed."

Darcy sighed. "There were quite a few Christmases done in such a way," he informed her.

"Faith, there was," Christmas Past said, "now let us look at another Christmas."

The room remained the same, but time performed its dance as the younger Darcy grew larger, indicating that seven years had gone by, and now Darcy was a teenager.

As he was ushered into the room, he was no longer the only child, because his mother and father entered the house having just arrived with a little girl.

It was Darcy's younger sister, Georgiana, who was five years old, and idolized her older brother, to the point of hero worship. Rather than be discomforted by this, Darcy enjoyed the idea that his little sister adored him so much, as well as that he could order her to do something, and she jumped at it. Many an older sibling enjoys it when they can do that, be it right or wrong.

"Georgiana!" Darcy cried, "when you were so little!"

Next, he sighed and looked at the ghost.

"Indeed, she cannot see or hear me. Georgiana made the Christmas holidays at Rosings Park more bearable. This was back when things were perfect, before Georgiana married, left England, and split up the family."

"She never forgot you," the spirit said.

"Family is everything. Family stays together. That's the rule that we were raised on. It keeps our family strong."

"Quiet and attend," Past ordered him, "I am trying to listen."

They directed their attention back to the scene of the Darcys, who had just arrived, and the servants were taking their coats, hats, comforters, and gloves.

"Is it really fair that we have to come to Rosings every Christmas, and Aunt Catherine never comes to Pemberley?" Georgiana asked her parents and her brother.

"I agree, Georgiana," the young Darcy said, "but because of Anne's bad health, she cannot travel far, and it prevents her from leaving Rosings Park."

When hearing mention of Anne de Bourgh, Georgiana gave Darcy a 'I know what everyone wants you both to do' look. It was teasing and was the equivalent of when someone less proper would stick their tongue out at you.

"Ah, right!" Georgiana laughed. "And Anne must not fall ill, Fitzy? Because we know what that means for you."

"Shut it," Darcy said, nudging her with his arm. "I do not want to hear it from you as well."

"Nor do I want to hear it from either of you," their father reprimanded, "hush now, and speak properly."

Georgiana and her brother fell in line, quickly.

"Yes, Father," young Darcy agreed.

"Sorry, Father," Georgiana said.

They entered a sitting room, where Lady Catherine met them, in all her festive glory. After many warm affections offered on both sides, and 'many merry Christmas' was said around, Lady Catherine immediately informed them all that there was going to be a dinner party that night, and there would be a ball at Crisham Hall, a neighboring estate in Kent, and she agreed that they would all be present.

"Ah," Darcy sighed to the spirit. "The Crisham Ball. It was the first ball that I had ever gone to."

"Did you enjoy yourself?" the Ghost asked.

"I was ordered, by my mother and my aunt, that I would dance with Cousin Anne for the first two dances. She barely spoke to me the entire time. Yet, that was not the worst of it."

"I know, because I believe, this is the worst you encountered."

The scene shifted to an hour later, and Lady Catherine was sitting down, when she ordered Fitzy to come to her side. The young Darcy sighed inwardly as he approached her and stood at attention.

"Yes, Aunt?"

"Tomorrow is the Crisham ball," she said, "and as you know, your cousin Anne, is delicate."

"I am aware of that, Aunt."

"But not delicate in the improper way," she declared, "but in the way that she would make a perfect wife. As you shall know, since you both are intended for each other, and will make a splendid pair."

When hearing this, young Darcy still did not respond,

despite every instinct that he had to run from the room. Yet more and more, he felt the pain of his fate being sealed.

"You were still a child and not royalty," Christmas Past acknowledged.

"That did not mean anything when it came to our legacy," Darcy replied.

"Well," Lady Catherine continued saying to her nephew, "since Anne will need your assistance, she will dance with you for the first two dances."

"She shall?"

"Yes, she shall, and you both are guaranteed to have a perfect time of it. However, she is having difficulty in practicing her dance movements. You and she must go to the music room, where there is plenty of space, Mrs. Jenkinson will play for you both, so that Anne will know all. She will be perfect for the event, because my Anne is perfect in all things, as you have suspected."

Having been ordered to the music room, Georgiana offered to go with him. Happy to have someone with him, young Darcy asked if she would permit this, and the adults agreed.

"She always wanted to be with me," Darcy told the spirit about Georgiana, "because she knew that it would help."

"Your sister has a large heart for so small a creature."

"Yes, Ghost. She does."

When the two siblings left the room, Darcy and Christmas Past followed them.

"Fitzy," Georgiana asked her brother.

"Yes?"

"Do you really have to marry our cousin? You must marry Anne?"

"Well—it's complicated," young Darcy answered.

"What does that mean?"

"Our aunt wants it. Our mother wants it, and our dad is not averse to the prospect. As such, I must commit to it."

"But must you? Why does it have to happen? And if this can happen to you, can it happen to me?"

Her brother looked down at her, affectionately. "You are the younger one. I do not think that they shall force you into an alliance that you do not want."

Georgiana smiled as she intentionally knocked into her brother.

"Good!" she cried. "I never want to get married. Boys are ugly."

"We are not ugly!"

"Yes, some of you are. And you smell strange."

"You smell stranger!"

"No, you do!"

"No, you do!"

Eventually, they arrived at the music room, and met Anne de Bourgh and Mrs. Jenkinson there, where the cousins were forced to be each other's dance partners.

If the ball had proven to be difficult, then so was the practice.

Not only did Anne de Bourgh have difficulty with the steps, it made her exhausted and soon, she gave up in frustration.

"Since she was my dance partner for an entire hour the next evening," Darcy explained to the ghost, "it proved to be humiliating, and the hardest hour of my life. It led to me barely caring for balls after that."

The Ghost of Christmas Past smiled but shook her head.

"Perhaps you developed a distaste for the event, at first, but there is one ball that you particularly enjoyed. Forgive me, I am getting ahead of myself. For let us look at Christmas day…

After the day was over, night had fallen, and young Darcy was in his room in bed, reading until he could fall asleep.

The ghost and his older self were standing in the shadows, by the window.

"I remember this night," Darcy said to the apparition. "Poor boy. Poor mother."

When hearing some footsteps stop at his door, young Darcy lowered his book, a little uneasy at how ominous the footsteps sounded.

Then there was a gentle knock, and its meekness put him at ease.

"Fitz," his mother said, "are you awake?"

"I am, Mama."

The door opened, and Mrs. Darcy entered, in her dressing gown, with her chemise under it and wearing slippers and a mop cap.

When seeing his mother, Darcy noted how, in the moonlight, how beautiful she was. Even though what she would say would heavily affect him, he found that he could never despise her.

"I thought you would be awake," she said, closing the

door behind her. She crossed to the bed, sat next to him and took his hand in hers.

Out of a desire to get closer to her, Darcy moved away from Christmas Past and sat down on the other side of the bed.

"Son," Mrs. Darcy said, "I wish to tell you how proud that I am of you. And how wonderful you were for dancing with your cousin for the whole hour at the ball."

Darcy looked down at his lap, and placed his book harshly on the bed, next to him. His mother knew what that meant.

"I know that it was a little mortifying," Mrs. Darcy elaborated.

"She kept turning the wrong way and colliding into me," Young Darcy explained. "Why was she made to dance when she was not ready?"

"My sister has high hopes for her, and this time, your Aunt Catherine believed her to be ready. But I can assure you that this is not the end of the world, and when you and Anne dance again, it will be better. You and she shall have many chances to bloom together."

Young Darcy rolled his head, uneasy and pained.

"Mama, we do not favor each other, and I do not think —I do not think that I can love her."

Mrs. Darcy placed a strand of hair behind her ear that had come down.

"My love, you are full young, and you do not know what the future may hold. Right now, you might not feel for her, but time can change many things."

She touched her son's cheek with affection.

"Sometimes, love can be found on the way to matrimony. Also, a marriage is more than just based on passions. It is based on similar qualities, and situations. You and Anne are of the same age and are in the same circle. By you both marrying, you unite Pemberley and Rosings Park. Between the estate, and the wealth, being joined, the alliance will make our families even more one of the strongest of England. You will have secured your family and all your descendants for generations. So much will be saved by this. You're at an age where you do not see it now, but with time comes wisdom."

Once more, young Darcy looked down at his lap, feeling hopeless under the weight of his family's wishes.

"Family, my son, is everything," she stressed. "Also, you know your cousin. Anne is meek, sickly, and dare I say it, weak because of my sister's strong will over her. If my niece were to marry, the husband could very easily intimidate her, be wholly inattentive to her, and dismiss any wish that she would make. She would be vulnerable to the whims of someone who might take advantage of her. But with you, being such a wonderful boy, you would not press your influence. You would not be abusive to her wishes. You are Anne's best hope."

Once more, she squeezed her son's hand.

"Fitz, for me," she implored, "consider that I am right. I love you so much, for a woman could not have wanted a better son."

"Mama," younger and older Darcy said together. When seeing their mother bestowing her affection on them, they weakened.

Mrs. Darcy kissed her son on the cheek.

"You are the best of men, you know," she said, "I know that no matter what you will do the right thing."

She left the room.

Once she closed the door behind her, the room remained, but everything else faded away, and it was just Darcy and the ghost.

"She loved me," Darcy said, still sitting on the bed.

"Yes, she did," Christmas Past said.

"That's why I could forgive her for everything. Because, whatever happened, her love for me was real."

"Real love," Christmas Past pointed out, "how long it has been since you have given way to that."

Christmas Past pointed to the book, it levitated, opened again and emitted a powerful light.

"Now, we go to another Christmastime."

The illumination covered them, once more, and they were hurled through time and space.

CHAPTER 6

Christmastime in Hertfordshire

W hen they materialized again from out of the book, they emerged on the front steps of a home in Hertfordshire County.

Darcy looked around on the steps while Christmas Past only looked ahead.

"I believe that you know this place," she uttered.

When recognizing it, and the landscape around it, it overwhelmed the Master of Pemberley, as he collapsed on the front steps, astonished.

"Know it," Darcy responded, "I could walk it blindfolded, with how much I walked up and down the green, in the brief time that I was here."

"Yes, Darcy," Past said, as she wrapped her cloak around herself that had materialized from thin air. "Welcome back to Netherfield Park."

Hearing the name, he felt a great release as he prepared to walk down moments of his history that he both dreaded as well as anticipated.

"I know," Darcy said to the ghost, "I know what I am

about to face."

"Yes, you do," the spirit responded, "but it doesn't change that you shall relive it, nevertheless. Do not look away, man, but walk down it again."

"I both do," Darcy said, "and also do not wish to, altogether."

"To dread your past as well as miss it; a common tendency of humanity. Do you know what day it is, and what is about to happen?"

At first, Darcy was confused, but in a flash, the answer came to him, from where he knew not how.

"This is the day that Bingley brought me, Mr. Hurst and his sisters to the house he rented."

As if his words summoned the event, a carriage and two horsemen were riding down the road and turning onto Netherfield lane.

Darcy saw his younger self, now fully grown, on one horse, and Bingley in the other.

The carriage parked in front of the steps, servants rushed from the home, through himself and the ghost, to attend to their master.

The carriage door opened, and Mr. Hurst, Mr. Bingley's brother-in-law, stepped out of the carriage. Next, he turned around and handed down Mr. Bingley's two sisters, Caroline Bingley, and Lousia Hurst.

With this new arrival, Darcy was not curious about his younger self, or the rest of the family for that matter. His eyes rested on Bingley—of Bingley of old, when he still had an open face, a warm smile, a kind nature, and a spirit that still was not forlorn.

He was Bingley before Bingley had been broken.

"What do you think?" Bingley asked Darcy. "I know that there were other options, but I do believe that this house is precisely what my father would have purchased if he were alive now."

"While I do not agree that your particular taste should depend *solely* on what your father would have wanted," Darcy acknowledged, "I do understand the need for doing one's duty. Since you wrote that all in the house is in working order, I think you made a good bargain when you rented this place. However, once you meet more of the county folk and families in this region, only then should you desire to fully purchase it."

"And I am not certain that you fully ought to," Caroline said. "I agree wholeheartedly with Mr. Darcy. This place is so far away from what I think you would desire, Charles."

"And the people are unlikely to be very fashionable," Louisa said, "especially being so far from town."

"From the little that I have seen, I enjoy the manners of the local gentry," Bingley said, walking up the steps, "and we arrived at the perfect time to meet everyone."

"Why?" Darcy asked, following him. "We must not be put on display, for I despise it."

"I should never put you through such a spectacle," Bingley said, now fully facing the older Darcy, who had no consciousness of him. "I know that you would detest that. We arrived at the precise time that they shall have an assembly. That way, we will meet everyone."

"A ball," Darcy said, rolling his eyes, "god preserve us."

As the family walked into the house, Bingley's face had grown so near to Darcy's invisible form, that he could see every physical detail of his old friend.

A flood of memories reached Darcy as he recalled all the days he and Bingley traveled and had many adventures together.

His heart felt a pang in it as Bingley, his younger self, and the sisters moved right through him and entered Netherfield.

When he was alone on the steps with the spirit, Darcy felt the familiar sensations of friendship, something he had not experienced for so long.

"What are you feeling?" the ghost asked him.

"Nothing."

"You miss having Bingley as a friend, even though it was you who destroyed the connections."

Darcy looked away, and at the green fields that stretched beyond, to the horizon.

"You have mocked me before, shade, and I asked not to do so again." Darcy glared at the spirit. "Do not mock me."

"I do not. These are the shadows of the things that have been. That they are what they are, do not blame me, especially because they are what you wish to see. Or because of who you are about to see."

Darcy continued to look ahead.

"The assembly," Darcy said.

"Yes," Christmas Past said, opening the book again.

This time, Darcy was not frightened nor bewildered. He was growing accustomed to being conducted where the spirit would take him.

When they were hurled out of the book, Darcy and the ghost appeared again, in a corner of the Assembly room in Meryton.

All the major families were in attendance, and the dance had already begun.

When Darcy had found his footing back on the floor, he moved in front of the ghost, to get a better view of who was there.

"You deprive me of a view," the ghost said.

"I cannot care just now," Darcy said, studying every face in the crowd.

Every woman was not the woman he sought.

"She must be here," Darcy hissed, moving forward, gliding through the dancers who had been doing the country dance.

He went back and forth until he heard a familiar voice.

It was Mrs. Bennet, the mistress of Longbourn, and mother to five daughters. Where she was, the daughters could not be far away.

Gliding through the crowd, he was surprised to find that Mrs. Bennet would be the face that he wanted to see. The pursuit had paid off, because three of her five daughters were with her, while the two others had been dancing.

And furthest down the set of ladies was one sister, whose back was to him. She was talking with another lady who resided in Hertfordshire, and that was Charlotte Lucas.

Despite not facing him, he knew her.

For she marked the face of the woman who he could never forget.

And ought to never forget.

"Turn around," Darcy whispered, aware that she couldn't hear him. "Turn around and look upon me."

"Lizzy and Jane," Mrs. Bennet said, "a carriage has just arrived, and I think it's the Netherfield Party."

This forced the young woman to turn around, and there she was.

"Elizabeth!" Darcy gasped.

There stood Elizabeth Bennet, the second of the five Bennet sisters, who would change his and Bingley's lives forever.

Darcy was rooted to the spot.

There was the face that launched a thousand sensations in his heart.

From her curly hair to her sparkling and intelligent eyes, and flattering face and figure, there marked a clever and superior mind underneath it all.

How many years had he not looked at her face, and Darcy now felt the distance of those days being separate from his life.

Slowly, he walked up to her, while she was wholly unaware of his shadow that was so close to her form.

Despite being unable to touch Elizabeth, Darcy raised up his arm and tried to press his fingers on her cheek.

Just the *thought* of touching her again…

Elizabeth moved through him as her mother pulled Elizabeth and Jane along, just as five people entered the assembly room. The music died down as three men and two women, all dressed handsomely, had entered.

An animated and jovial man, named Sir William Lucas,

who owned the estate of Lucas Lodge, refused to let awkwardness ensue.

Darcy watched as his younger self, Bingley, and his sisters, awkwardly stood there, as Sir William approached them and welcomed them to our assembly.

"I remember that moment," Darcy said to the ghost, "I found Sir William's behavior to be filled with self-importance."

"Because he cared enough to welcome you?" she responded. "Because he is possessed by the fountain of human kindness? What a sin, eh?"

Still, Darcy did not draw closer to his younger self and the Netherfield Party.

He remained closer to Elizabeth who was looking at the newcomers who were in their midst.

Now that he was able to see things from another perspective—from the point of view that the spirit had bestowed on him—he could then see that Eliza was looking at one person in the group of newcomers.

"Me," Darcy uttered, "she was looking upon me."

"Precisely," the spirit said, "she was looking at you."

Darcy followed her gaze and saw his younger self.

In his earlier figure, Darcy saw the haughty expression, and how he looked positively dismal and grim.

Everything about his appearance said, 'do not approach me'.

And all the while, Elizabeth had condescended to look at him, when he was not doing so.

"She was looking at me when I was looking everywhere else, but at her," Darcy said, but the ghost said nothing. He looked at his younger self with disdain. "You imbecile!

From the very beginning, you limited our chances with her."

Then he realized that he was chastising himself.

"But I was the fool," Darcy realized.

As the night wore on, Darcy experienced another sensation of watching his memories unfold before him.

Humiliation!

Throughout the assembly, Darcy had to experience how much his friend was favored, and he was ill-favored. Bingley ingratiated himself with the entire room, danced every dance, regretted how early the ball was over, and vowed to do one of his own.

It was certain that Bingley was sure to be liked from wherever he went, while Darcy was accused of causing offense.

Darcy watched as his younger self walked here, walked there, showed a definite refusal to become acquainted with people, was offended when others addressed him, and was determined not to stand up with anyone but the women from his own party.

Such particular attention to dance with Caroline Bingley also made Darcy question his conduct to her as well. Making her his particular partner naturally flattered Caroline and made her wonder about him becoming her husband.

Even worse, Darcy overheard many people snigger, criticizing his younger self, and he had to suffer the snide remarks of how they all didn't like him.

Despite Darcy's cold and biting manner, he was showing himself to not be made of stone. And no matter what anyone claims... words hurt.

Eventually, Darcy had no choice but to watch an old scene that would always cause him pain: when he and Elizabeth first officially acknowledged each other. All he could do was sit there and watch the scene unfold as it occurred:

His former self was standing aloof, while Caroline Bingley and Mrs. Hurst were dancing with other gentlemen.

Elizabeth Bennet had been obliged, by the scarcity of men, to sit down for two dances. During that time, Mr. Darcy's former self had been standing near enough for her to overhear a conversation between him and Mr. Bingley, who came from the dance for a few minutes, to press his friend to join it.

"Come, Darcy. I must have you dance. I hate to see you standing about, by yourself, in this stupid manner. You had much better dance."

"I certainly shall not. Excepting your sisters, I do not feel a comfort in standing up with anyone else. The idea of choosing another would not do at all. At an assembly such as this, it would be unsupportable, even a punishment for me to stand up with anyone else."

"I would not be nearly as taciturn and obstinate as you, for a kingdom," Bingley protested. "The ladies in the company are very pleasant, agreeable, and several of them very lovely!"

During this moment, Bingley focused his gaze on Jane Bennet, the eldest Bennet sister to Longbourn. She had a reputation for being the loveliest of women in the county.

Even the former Darcy could not deny this.

"You have been dancing with the only handsome girl in the room."

When seeing that his friend was willing to agree with him, Bingley was able to speak his opinion more animatedly.

"Oh, she is, without doubt, the most beautiful creature that I ever beheld. Yet, I cannot agree with you that she is the *only* handsome woman in the room. Beauty is not a singular thing, after all. For example, look just over there," Bingley gestured to Elizabeth Bennet. Darcy echoed the action, took a quick look at Elizabeth before he turned his nose up at her and looked away.

Darcy watched his former self, in agony.

"There is one of her sisters sitting down over there. She is very pretty, and I dare say, very agreeable. Do let me ask my partner to introduce you."

"She is tolerable, to an extent," his younger self responded, "but not nearly handsome enough to tempt me. And I am in no humor to give consequence to young ladies who have been slighted by other men. Return to your partner, enjoy her smiles, as I know that you shall. Yet with me, I shall do as I do, and there's an end on it."

"Very well," Bingley responded, "I shall leave you to the wall."

Bingley walked off, leaving former Darcy to remain with his pride for company, and Elizabeth Bennet to overhear how she had been slighted.

Darcy rushed up to his former self, drew his face close to his, and snapped at him.

"You blind imbecile," he declared, "can you not see that she is the most handsome woman of your acquaintance? It always took you too long."

Leaning back, and looking at Christmas Past, he realized that he was criticizing himself. Again.

Rolling his head back, he sighed.

"With her, I always took way too long," he realized.

"Yes," Christmas Past replied, "indeed you did."

The scene dissolved and the two of them were left in black.

Christmas Past rolled her hand, the book levitated in the air and the pages began to turn.

With each turning of the page a quick scene erupted around them, of days going by where Mr. Darcy encountered Elizabeth.

First, it was a quick flash of when she paid the Bingley sisters a visit with her family.

A page turned…

Second, Darcy and the Netherfield party had been invited to a dinner at Lucas Lodge, and Darcy's former self spied Elizabeth talking to Charlotte Lucas.

He admired the manner and animation that came to her eyes when she would laugh at something that was said.

A page turned…

He was riding his horse along a field, stopping his horse near the end of a meadow, when he saw a figure running through the woods that neared it.

The woman was ignorant of his presence, but he watched her run along, enjoying the activity.

It was Elizabeth Bennet. He watched her until she disappeared from sight.

A page turned…

Darcy and the Netherfield company had been invited to a dinner party at Lucas Lodge.

While there, Elizabeth Bennet had been asked to play at the pianoforte. She had performed two songs, and despite not being perfect in music or voice, Darcy found himself unable to take his eyes off her.

Rather, he moved to another side of the throng, to get a better view of her.

The page turned…

Elizabeth's younger sister, Mary, who was regarded as the plainest of the group, had been asked to play some Scottish and Irish airs, so the company could dance.

Darcy watched his former self still standing in the corner, being talked to by Sir William Lucas, being wholly inattentive to his host's congenial words.

"While part of your cold manner can be attributed to pride and a sardonic humor," Christmas Past asked Darcy, "is there any possibility that you are merely shy… bashful?"

Darcy did not respond.

"Would it have just been so hard to explain that to people?" Christmas past furthered.

Darcy's jaw was even more set.

"A man should not walk about displaying his habits," he professed. "They did not deserve an explanation."

"Why did Sir William Lucas not deserve it?"

"He was beneath me."

Christmas Past looked strongly at him, and a light radiated from her to such a degree, that Darcy shirked and shook.

"*No one* is beneath *anyone*," Christmas Past said, simply, but strongly. It is difficult to not raise one's voice while still being ferocious, but the spirit achieved it flawlessly.

Darcy did not respond, and just as well, because he then saw his former self glimpse Elizabeth, who had just walked past them both. Sir William, wishing to be gallant, stopped Elizabeth in her tracks.

"My dear Miss Eliza, why are you not dancing?" He gestured to Mr. Darcy's former self. "Mr. Darcy, you must allow me to present this young lady to you as a very desirable partner—you cannot refuse to dance, I am sure, when so much beauty is before you."

Since Darcy had relived this, he knew her answer, and understood why.

"Indeed, sir, I have not the least intention of dancing— I entreat you not to suppose that I moved this way in order to *beg* for a partner."

"I would be very happy if you were to stand up with me, Miss Elizabeth, for this dance," Mr. Darcy's former self said gravely.

"Mr. Darcy is all politeness—*at present*," Elizabeth Bennet said, "yet, wishing to dance requires two who enjoy the activity. Since earlier, Mr. Darcy views dancing as a compliment which he never pays to any place if he can avoid it, I do not wish to go where angels dare to tread. That would not be a pleasant experience for the gentleman, now would it?"

With that, Elizabeth turned away, took two steps, and watched as Darcy's former self had a sudden impulse to call after her.

"Perhaps this opportunity could be deferred," Darcy

stated gravely, but strongly. "For another time. Another dance—perhaps."

Not knowing what to make of his speech, Elizabeth's eyes shifted back and forth, then she nodded her head and departed.

The page turned…

It was another day, and another interesting development that occurred when Darcy's former self was sitting in the dining room, along with Bingley's family, during breakfast time.

He had recently learned that Jane Bennet, Elizabeth's sister, was resting in a guest room, having fallen ill on her visit with the Bingley sisters.

Throughout most of the meal, Darcy watched as his former self ate, did not offer much discussion, but only listened.

"He's wondering," Darcy explained to the spirit, "since Jane Bennet was recovering at Netherfield, that perhaps Elizabeth would come to see to her sister."

"You meant that '*you* are wondering if she would come'."

"Same difference."

"Ah. And you were satisfied…"

The page turned…

Darcy and the ghost materialized right in the middle of the town, Meryton, which was a few miles from Elizabeth's home, Longbourn.

When they landed, it was amidst a street where Darcy was right in front of a cart that was riding along.

He flinched and cowered as the horse and cart rode

right through him, went about his natural course, and Darcy was unscathed.

Christmas Past could not help but chuckle.

"I suppose that you enjoyed that," Darcy said, wiping down his clothes, as if he had dirt on them.

"I did," the shade replied, "enormously."

When hearing familiar laughs, Darcy turned around and saw that Elizabeth was walking with her sisters, Kitty and Lydia.

Kitty and Lydia said farewell to Lizzy, who were going to call on some soldiers' wives. They told her to give Jane their regards and hope that she was well.

Elizabeth began to walk in the other direction.

"I know this moment," Darcy said, "this must've been when she was about to walk to Netherfield Park, to stay with Jane. She is going to see her sister. I was not there, but I know this must be the moment."

"Then let us travel to when she arrives," Past offered, raising up the book again.

"No!" Darcy implored her. Not harshly, but pleadingly. "Let me walk with her. Please! I always wondered about it, even if she cannot see me, I shall not be bored. And you are a spirit; you have all the time in the world, which I have not. Please, let me walk with her."

At first, the spirit only looked at him.

"Please!" Darcy urged. "I ask for little."

Christmas Past made her decision, and closed the book, which was as good a sign as any.

"Thank you," Darcy said.

"I shall see you in due course," Past said, "now go. For you must catch up with her."

Christmas Past vanished, leaving Darcy to run and follow the love of his life.

At first, he walked quickly.

Yet, as Caroline Bingley once described, Elizabeth Bennet must be allowed to be a great walker. For which she was. Darcy's casual footfalls were not enough to catch up with her, therefore he did something unprecedented: he began to run.

Past labor men, past shopkeepers, he ran.

Past people walking about with their children, past servants rushing to get places, he ran.

Winded, he felt exhausted, but also enlivened. He discovered a newfound energy that one does not have the pleasure to experience when their lives are filled with servants having to do everything, for the sake of maintaining a 'respectable lifestyle'.

However, Darcy was invisible, not spied on by society or by the constant watch of those who tended to him. This gave him the ability to be…free.

Eventually, all obstacles cleared before him, and he reached Elizabeth's back.

Slowing down, he caught his breath and walked behind her at first.

Eventually, he gathered his nerve and walked alongside her. Looking around the side of her bonnet, he was able to see her face.

Without fear of appearing rude, he could look all that he preferred and marked every angle of her features.

Just like it had been before, he realized the beauty of her, the unique quality that many ladies have. It's a loveliness that goes undetected when you first see them; but after two or three encounters, you see their pulchritude, that special aspect that makes them glow. Elizabeth had it, and it cast a spell over him, leaving him entirely bewitched.

When she crossed fields, he remained by her side, going at a quick pace.

She jumped over stiles and springing over puddles with impatient activity, to the point where Darcy could barely keep up.

When she accidentally stepped into a muddy patch, it led to her boots and hem of her gown being dirtied.

"Miss Bingley will abuse you for that," Darcy uttered, amused.

"I shall get abused for that," Elizabeth muttered to herself.

Darcy could not help but smile at the coincidence of them having the same thought.

Even though she could not see him, it didn't matter. He cherished every moment with her, until Netherfield Park came into view.

Suddenly, Christmas Past appeared right next to him, tapped him on the shoulder and Darcy and she disappeared from Elizabeth's side.

When he opened his eyes again, he was upstairs, watching his former self in the music room, practicing.

While his sister was an accomplished talent at the pianoforte, it was a lesser-known fact that Darcy had also learned to play. He was, by no means, a master. Yet he was accomplished enough to still have the ability. Seeking the comfort of being alone, his former self sat down to the instrument and was playing a Scottish air, when he noticed a figure crossing the field.

From where younger Darcy was placed, he faced a window which gave him the perfect view of the green.

Recognizing the lady, Darcy's former self stopped playing, walked over to the window, and gazed out of it.

There, across the grass, was Elizabeth Bennet.

"She's walking?" Younger Darcy uttered, amazed. "She clearly walked here."

With that, Darcy's younger self adjusted his waistcoat, put on his jacket, and walked out of the music room.

Darcy, with the ghost behind him, watched Elizabeth come up the field, and approach the front steps to the house.

"You admired her for walking that distance," the ghost said.

"Yes. Even when I stated the contrary."

The scene shifted to when Elizabeth Bennet did arrive. She was shown into the breakfast parlor, where the entire family was assembled, except for Jane.

Many comments were made concerning her walking three miles so early in the day, in such dirty weather, and by herself was almost incredible to the Bingley sisters.

Mr. Bingley was kind and Mr. Darcy's former self was too amazed to know what to fully say.

While he was never in doubt that Elizabeth would eventually come, he was surprised she came so quickly. It caught him unawares. Whatever he had planned on how to enhance his relationship with her, now abandoned him, due to lack of preparation.

When she entered, Elizabeth did look upon Mr. Darcy's former self, who bowed to her, but the only satisfaction he got was that lingering look.

After inquiring about Jane's ill health, Elizabeth was sent to tend to her older sister immediately.

"She spent the whole day looking after Miss Bennet," Darcy informed the spirit. "When it was time for dinner, I was happy to see her near me again."

"Near you?" Past said. "That's how it all began."

The page turned…

CHAPTER 7

The Pages Turn, & Time
with It

S ince Elizabeth had come to tend to her sister, it still
was natural—more so required—to sit with the family
for some time during and after dinners. As a result, she
changed into some clothes for dinner, came downstairs, and
joined the Netherfield Party in the drawing room.

Elizabeth took up some needlework, while the rest were
occupied in different directions.

Mr. Darcy's former self was sitting away from the
group, writing a letter.

Mr. Hurst and Mr. Bingley were at piquet.

Mrs. Hurst was observing their game.

Yet, Caroline Bingley was the only one who's behavior
proved intrusive and ill-conceived. As is natural when
someone fancies anyone, and the feeling is not reciprocated,
the best thing would be to leave the object of their affections alone. However, that is not always the initial reaction.
Rather, it is a natural, though illogical, tendency to try
one's best to push our company on them more, in hopes to

get noticed. Simply put, it is a habit to '*try too hard*'. It's a sad practice that many a person has fallen into.

Caroline Bingley, sadly, was no different than many a human and had caught the disease that renders us as, 'oppressively overbearing'.

As Darcy's former self was writing his letter, Caroline revolved around him, like a moth to a flame.

Christmas Past and Darcy were standing by a window in the room, giving them ample view to see everything.

Darcy, as was his habit, gravitated toward where Elizabeth was.

"She was watching how Caroline pursued me," Darcy observed, "and saw me as an object to have and to hold. Life would have been simpler to have married Miss Bingley. She certainly would have believed so, but *love* got in the way. And then *duty* got in the way of love."

"Yes," Christmas Past said, "that is the step you took. Now attend, so you can see the difference between the ladies; one who wished to obtain you, and the one who made no such attempt."

Though focused on her needlework, Elizabeth could split her attention and she watched poor Miss Bingley and her perpetual commendations on Darcy's handwriting, or on the evenness of his lines, or on the length of his letter, with the perfect unconcern with which her praises were received, formed a curious dialogue, and was exactly in unison with Elizabeth's opinion of each.

"How delighted Miss Darcy will be to receive such a letter!" Miss Bingley remarked.

He made no answer.

"You write uncommonly fast."

"You are mistaken. I write rather slowly."

"How many letters you must have occasion to write in the course of a year! Letters of business, too! How odious I should think them!"

"It is fortunate, then, that they fall to my lot instead of to yours."

"Pray tell your sister that I long to see her."

"I have already told her so once, by your desire."

"I am afraid you do not like your pen. Let me mend it for you. I mend pens remarkably well."

"Thank you—but I always mend my own."

"How can you contrive to write so even?"

He was silent.

"Tell your sister I am delighted to hear of her improvement on the harp and pray let her know that I am quite in raptures with her beautiful little design for a table, and I think it infinitely superior to Miss Grantley's."

"Will you give me leave to defer your raptures till I write again? At present I have not room to do them justice."

"Oh, it is of no consequence. I shall see her in January. But do you always write such charming long letters to her, Mr. Darcy?"

"They are generally long; but whether always charming, it is not for me to determine."

"It is a rule with me, that a person who can write a long letter with ease cannot write ill."

Elizabeth chuckled briefly, suppressed a smile, and returned to sewing.

Darcy smiled.

"What she must have thought of me," Darcy

mentioned to the ghost. "I know it. She viewed me as a taciturn and discontented fellow, and that Miss Bingley was an officious and relentless seeker."

"She was correct," the spirit said of Elizabeth.

"Yes, she was," Darcy said, his eyes growing misty. "Elizabeth was correct about many things."

The page turned again…

After a couple more days when Elizabeth remained at Netherfield Park, tending to Jane, Mr. Darcy was in the library. And so was Elizabeth.

The coincidence was real, for Younger Darcy knew that she had finished her book and needed a different one. As she walked into the room, she was startled to find him sitting there, reading near a desk.

When she looked at him, Darcy stood up and bowed.

"We both find ourselves in need of a good book, Miss Bennet."

"Indeed, we do, sir. However, I am as much not a town crier, as much as I am not a dormouse: I will not disturb your privacy with my presence. I shall get my book, return to my sister's room, and you shall hear no more of me."

At first, Darcy's former self nodded, but remained standing. He watched as Elizabeth searched through the shelves.

Unwilling to sit still any further, Darcy's former self closed his book, walked to a shelf near Elizabeth, slowly removed the book from where it was placed and handed it to her.

"I think you will find this book very fascinating," Darcy said, "I would recommend it."

"Mr. Darcy is being polite again," Elizabeth responded,

looking at the book's title. "Now he gives me a recommendation. I am glad that it is not a conduct book, or I would have been tempted to rebel against your choice of books."

"I would never hand you something that you neither needed nor required."

"A gallant answer."

"A true answer," Darcy's former self stated. "Miss Bennet, I must ask you something."

"It's a free land to ask a question," Elizabeth responded, "yet I do not have to guarantee an answer if the question proves to be incongruous."

"Why did you not wish to dance with me at Lucas Lodge, for the dinner party?"

The question was finally asked.

It hung in the air, not because of Elizabeth's shame, but mere astonishment. Of course, that astonishment shifted to a slight indignation that was only masked by her arched and amusing expression.

"Why did I not dance with you?" Elizabeth repeated the question. "How surprising to hear such a query come from you. You, who does quite detest the activity, in general. I think the answer lies within you; do you not think?"

Elizabeth moved away, still holding the book, but Darcy narrowed the distance.

"What am I to think?"

"That you have a mind that perplexes me and confuses me," Elizabeth responded.

She did not back away from him, however, but maintained her ground as she continued.

"One moment, you are unhappy at the prospect of

dancing, and then you give in to Sir William's wishing to pair us. It does not seem incumbent upon me to dance with someone who would despise us dancing together. Firstly, you will be miserable, because you dislike dancing, and I shall be miserable by having a partner who is unhappy with the prospect. I would assume that you would thank me, for I spared us both from a tedious half-hour of each other's company. My logic is sound, from a point of view."

This time, it was Darcy's former self that had walked away from Elizabeth. Now there was some distance between them.

"And what is the second reason?" Younger Darcy asked. "I suspect that there is another one."

"Indeed, there is, and ought to be," Elizabeth pursued, walking up to him, "for surely you must understand that a lady has the right and power of refusal. It is one of the few luxuries that we can afford, regarding social etiquette."

Elizabeth placed her hands behind her back, and then she continued speaking.

"And also, if a gentleman is offered to dance with a woman, and *he flatly refuses* to stand up with her, then surely the lady can have a similar right? Correct? After all, if one is permissible and the other is unacceptable, then that shall place a double standard on the matter. And we would not want that, would we?"

"No, we would not."

Elizabeth moved back away from him and sat down briefly.

"I presume that this is a good novel that you have given me," she announced.

"I do believe that it is."

They remained there, with a distance between them.

"I think I can speak freely."

"I would, by no means, withhold any thought of yours," Elizabeth responded. "Since I have little opportunity of knowing the way in which your mind works."

"Miss Bennet, you may tell me if I am wrong, but I wish to know everything, in hopes that we can progress."

Elizabeth did not respond but merely nodded her head.

"Is our *present* course, by any means, inspired by our *past?*" When he asked this, Elizabeth looked at him, and then looked away. "I ask this because I want to give you clarity in the *future*. Is there any chance, when we first saw each other at the assembly, that you overheard my conversation with Mr. Bingley?"

"If you lay eavesdropping at my feet," Elizabeth pointed out, "then recall that there is no way to spy on a conversation displayed publicly, and very audibly."

"I shall not, but you did hear Bingley offer to introduce you to me and to have us dance. And I gather, that you heard my refusal."

"And the *manner* in which that refusal was bestowed," Elizabeth responded, leaning forward, and then standing up. "Do you plead guilty for being inconsiderate? Or are we about to banter?"

"You enjoy confrontation, I see?"

"On the contrary, I prefer peace. I merely do not *fear* confrontation. There is a difference. Woman, like man, must be able to speak for oneself."

"I can understand."

Elizabeth folded her arms over her chest.

"Well," she continued, "do you plead guilty, or no?"

"Guilty."

When hearing that, Elizabeth closed her eyes, smiled, and then opened them again.

"I am glad that you acknowledge it. Is there any way that, by the sword of King Arthur, that you realize that, perhaps, that was a little offensive."

"I do."

Darcy's former self took a step forward.

Elizabeth echoed the action.

"And that, I would like, and prefer, you to be kinder towards me, in the future."

"And I shall begin with the present. I begin now. Miss Bennet, my words were harsh, unjust, and ill-spoken. In truth, it was not that I was against the idea of dancing with you, or that I found your company reprehensible. For your part, you did nothing. For my part, I did everything. I was not in the best humor that evening. Rather, I disdained the idea of going out, to an assembly, and nothing could have made me anything less than disagreeable."

"Why?" Elizabeth asked. "Unless it is too intrusive to ask, what caused your unhappy manner."

"I—" Darcy's former self rubbed his forehead, insecure. "I have not that talent of conversing easily with people that I have never met before. I am—"

"Shy?"

When hearing the word, Darcy looked at the floor.

"It is no sin to admit to this trait," Elizabeth said, "because by admitting it, it helps us understand you better. All of Hertfordshire will forgive you, even with your bashful ways, because they know you better. No one can forgive a bitter disposition, if not given an explanation behind it."

"There," Christmas Past said to Darcy, "in Elizabeth's case, you did explain yourself. And look what it brought you."

Darcy did not respond, but watched his past unfold.

"Therefore," Elizabeth continued to Darcy's former self, "are you somewhat bashful?"

"Yes, I am," former Darcy confessed, "when being around people who I have made little to no acquaintance with, puts me out of humor easily. Yet, I do believe that I do improve on further acquaintance. I just need time, if you can accept that, as well as my apology?"

"Well," Elizabeth said, taking another step forward, "it would be most indelicate not to accept an apology that is properly given."

"It would be," he replied, taking a step toward her.

"Very well. I thank you for the apology, and I hope… that we shall see each other with less cruel things to say to one another."

"I would prefer that. And if I were to ask you to dance with me, would you accept my hand? I have seen you dance, and I found you to be a remarkable dancer."

"You think me worthy to dance with you?" Elizabeth asked, with an arched eyebrow, amused.

"No, it is the opposite," he responded, with a powerful intensity in his eye, "I finally have discovered that I am finally worthy enough to dance with you."

Elizabeth smiled and looked at the floor.

"I shall agree to that, as you can imagine. Forgive me if I am blushing. Blushing is a woman's trade which even I am prey to."

"It becomes you."

Elizabeth breathed in deeply, very overwhelmed by the sincere flattery. After spending so long casting biting remarks at each other, now the pendulum shifted, and Elizabeth didn't know what to do. Darcy's younger self was a little disorientated himself.

"You speak well," Elizabeth responded, "yet is it me, or did we do better at speaking cruelly to each other? In that, we knew what to say."

"Yes," he acknowledged, "it was easier."

"How strange we mortals be, that it is easier to be at odds with someone rather than to be even with them."

"It is a fault in how we are made, I do not deny. And yes, I think it was easier for us to throw volleys at each other and walk away enjoying it."

"Yes, to be uncommonly clever in taking so decided a dislike to someone, without any reason," Elizabeth furthered, walking away from him again and picking up the book.

"It is such a spur to one's genius," she continued, "such an opening for wit, to have a dislike of that kind. One may be continuously abusive without saying anything just. Yes, how strange we mortals be."

After a few seconds of reflection, Elizabeth turned back to Darcy.

"Yes," Elizabeth responded, "If you were to ask me to dance, I think that I shall dance with you again. And thank you for the book recommendation."

With that, she left the room.

Older Darcy watched her go.

"That was where it all began," he said to the ghost.

"And it only rose higher," Christmas Past said.

The page turned…

After Jane had recovered, she returned to Longbourn. Her company at Netherfield was missed by Mr. Bingley, but he was not the only man who felt that he lost valuable company.

Indeed, Mr. Darcy also felt the loss of Elizabeth that, as soon as was respectable, he joined Bingley in setting out to Longbourn, to inquire about Miss Bennet's health.

It gave Darcy the opportunity to see Elizabeth, while also being above suspicion. After all, to the outside world, he was merely joining Bingley. He had not committed himself, because he had no right to commit himself in any other direction than the one that had been destined for him.

He was told to marry Anne de Bourgh, so marry her, he perhaps ought to do.

Yet, with Elizabeth, there could be no harm in him liking an agreeable woman. After all, there was nothing wrong in being gentlemanlike, especially if you were a gentleman.

Therefore, Darcy and Christmas Past watched as Mrs. Bennet, in hopes of getting Mr. Bingley to marry her daughter, encouraged them to take a walk about the grounds.

Kitty and Lydia had already walked to Meryton and were not present, while Mary had to tend to her studies.

That naturally left Bingley and Darcy to walk with the two eldest Bennet sisters. From all directions, this was the best arrangement that could have occurred.

That left Mr. Bingley to walk with Jane and Darcy's former self to walk with Elizabeth.

Since the first set of couples had much to discuss, they naturally walked slower, in hopes of having a more intimate discussion.

"So," Elizabeth said, "that leaves us to find something to talk about while your friend and my sister walk through their entire life's story."

"If she is willing to convey such," Darcy said. "Forgive me, but sometimes I observe your sister and while Bingley is always overjoyed to see her, I wonder if she feels the same."

"What nonsense you speak, sir, and so early in the day. Jane prefers Mr. Bingley's company, always. Of that, I am certain."

"Yes," he said, a little dubious.

"You doubt me?" Elizabeth furthered. "I can see it in your eyes."

"I just wonder at it. When around him, she does enjoy his company, but I never see anything too marked—what I simply mean is that your sister is amenable and kind to everyone. With Bingley, how she is to him is how she is to anyone."

"That is the perfect way that it ought to be," Elizabeth surmised.

A couple strands of her hair fell, and she had to place it back before she continued.

"If you enjoy someone's company, and yield to the preference for them that you began to feel, it is best for it not to be discovered by the world, in general, because you are united with great strength of feeling, as well as a composure of temper and uniform cheerfulness of manner, that it would guard you from the suspicions of the impertinent."

Out of a desire to defend her sister, Elizabeth realized that she might have revealed a great deal too much.

"That is to say——" Elizabeth rushed out, "I am not saying one thing or the other about what Jane feels. Her feelings are her own, and I cannot reveal them, out of ignorance."

"Then… you are not certain of where her affections lay?"

Elizabeth looked ahead, trying to regulate her breathing.

"Even if I did," Elizabeth finalized, on hopes of covering her mistake, "I certainly shall not tell. A sister's prerogative, you must understand."

Darcy had no choice but to give in.

"Very well," Darcy assented, "it is."

"Precisely. You have a sister. Naturally, whatever she is feeling, you know the errors of putting those feelings out there for the world to see."

"No, indeed, I would not," Darcy declared.

"Precisely. That's a brother's love. A sister's love is no different."

"I yield to that logic," Darcy acknowledged, despite that he was unsatisfied. Since he had been watching Jane and Mr. Bingley from the first meeting, he studied them. Bingley liked Jane, undoubtedly. Yet with Jane, she was pleasant but also guarded. Her emotions are so concealed that Darcy was unaware if she had any deep feelings for his friend. Dearly, he should have liked Elizabeth to have told him so. Sadly, it was improper to inquire further, so he had to abandon the subject entirely.

"Speaking about sisters," Elizabeth furthered, "let us

speak of yours. All while I was at Netherfield Park, the Bingley sisters listed every virtue and ounce of perfection that Miss Darcy gives off. It must be wonderful to have a clever and ideal little sister."

"My sister has many fine qualities. I just wish that I was a better older brother to her sometimes."

Hearing Darcy's younger self speak so humbly sparked Elizabeth's interest.

"How so?" she asked. "I am not asking for the sake of pushing into your private feelings, but I thought it was only right to ask."

"I can unveil such, without giving away secrets. However, I am kind to her, attentive, and I care for her."

"I saw that when I was at Netherfield. You were writing a letter to your sister on the first night I was there. Miss Bingley adored her."

"She does, but it's strange. Sometimes, Miss Bingley's compliments are much appreciated, but sometimes they feel—"

"Heavy?" Elizabeth described.

"What do you refer to when you use the term?"

"Compliments are beautiful, for it is lovely to be kind, but too much praise can be overpowering. *Heavy.* And that's what I feel is occurring between you both. Her compliments are a delight, and then they can be dreadful. Forgive me for being harsh, but I speak merely as I find. My apologies if I am speaking too brown of Miss Bingley, but she and I have a way of being frank about the other."

"True. I cannot begrudge you for speaking as she has spoken."

"You are exhausted from civility, I daresay. Perhaps you

are overtired from officious attention and just want mere conversation." Elizabeth gave him a side glance. "Or am I wrong?"

"No, I do not think that you are," Darcy's former self admitted.

"You find me correct about something?" Elizabeth chuckled. "Heavens rejoice! He thinks that I am right about something."

Despite himself, Darcy smiled.

"And there it is," Elizabeth noted, "another miracle: you smiled. Note the time of day. Darcy smiled, which means, the world must be ending."

"You mock me," he stated.

"I tease you. There's a difference. And really, you must let me have one win here. After all, it's only a matter of time before you return to Derbyshire, or town. I have a small amount of time to see you happy before we part ways. Enjoy these days of levity, Mr. Darcy, before you return to the world of serious."

Darcy watched his former self stop in his tracks. This gave Elizabeth no choice but to stop as well.

"You look angry with me," Elizabeth said, unafraid.

"Yes, I am," he responded.

"Why? I thought we had been getting along splendidly."

"I just—"

"What?" Elizabeth said, turning to look at him. "I am here, and no words that you say can knock me down with a feather."

"I just want to know…"

"Yes?"

Elizabeth placed her finger behind her ear, in a teasing way to get him to speak up.

"I have given you your cue, now the audience is waiting for your line," Elizabeth responded.

"How do you see me?" he asked.

"How do I see you?"

"Yes."

"A very interesting question," Elizabeth wondered, becoming thoughtful. "Oh, a very forward one. Not offensive, but it leaves me a little confused of how to respond, because I never thought of it before. Give me a moment to reflect, so that I can give you something other than silence."

They walked to a swing that hung on the edge of the estate, and Elizabeth sat down on it.

"Do be seated," Elizabeth invited, "there is no impropriety behind it."

"Well, thank you," Darcy's former self said, then he sat down on the swing next to her.

"Are you prepared to answer now?" he asked.

"Well," Elizabeth began, "first, I see a man who is the friend of our new neighbor. I know that is a safe answer, but I am now just beginning."

"I am prepared."

"Thank you. Secondly, I do see you as the friend of the man who comes to see my sister a great deal."

"True."

"Now," Elizabeth said, looking toward the estate, "I see you as the man who it would be nice to get along with, and if he is willing, I should like to be his friend. If not, common and pleasant acquaintances would be still sufficient."

"You wish to be my *friend*?" Darcy asked, pointedly.

"If you let me. Understand, I put no prerequisites on you, or any pressure. We do not have to be friends if you do not wish. Nothing is being pressed. Yet, I should like to know you better if you let me."

"Oh," Darcy's younger self said, comprehension dawning, "I understand."

"You were worried," Christmas Past noted, "that she only wanted you as simply that, and no more."

"True, I was worried," Darcy responded to the ghost, "that she meant that she wanted to be my friend, and only that. When it became evident that it was the first sign to something greater that could form, I felt—"

"What?"

Darcy had felt elated, but he did not wish to utter it aloud, let alone to the spirit.

"It is no matter. Never mind."

They continued to watch the scene.

"Now is the hour of wonder," Elizabeth asked. "Could Mr. Darcy, of Pemberley, Derbyshire, see himself being friends with Elizabeth Bennet, of Longbourn, Hertfordshire?"

"There are few things that I am not in the humor to do, especially things that I prefer not to have my own way about."

"It's human to not want to do what they do not want to do. We all like to go our own way, I suppose. Does this mean that we are not friends?"

"Forgive me," he responded, "I waited too long to finish my thought. I should like us to be friends. And if you find me to be agreeable, I should like to call on you, whenever Bingley comes to visit Longbourn."

"Good," Elizabeth responded, "you might have to, because I doubt that I am going to be invited to Netherfield Park again. Unless, by some miracle, Jane falls ill on the property, and I have to make a three mile walk again."

"That's a long walk."

"It's not the mileage that I fear, but what comes afterwards. Now that we are friends, I can confess to something."

"What?"

Elizabeth leaned forward, conspiratorially. He leaned in, placing his ear nearer to her lips.

"I do not think that Miss Bingley and Mrs. Hurst like me at all."

"No, they don't," Darcy whispered back.

This led to Elizabeth laughing.

"Sorry," he said, lightly, "was I callous to tell you?"

"It would have hurt my vanity if my life was ruled by their opinion of me, but it is not. You are safe from me being hurt in hearing it, because you didn't say anything that I didn't know already."

They both laughed together.

Next, slowly, and naturally, without even thinking, they began to swing together.

At first, it was slow, with the wind brushing gently against their cheeks.

Then they swung higher and higher.

At the tree trunk where they were swinging from, Darcy and Christmas Past were still watching.

The Spirit gazed upon Darcy mildly. It's gentle touch

on Darcy's shoulder, though it had been light and instantaneous, appeared still present to the misanthrope's sense of feeling. Watching his younger self swinging with Elizabeth, in total agreement, Darcy was conscious of a thousand odors floating in the air, each one connected with a thousand thoughts, and hopes, and joys, and cares, long, long forgotten.

When it was time to return to the house so that younger Darcy and Bingley could offer their farewells to Mrs. Bennet, both couples had arrived at a delightful place of total agreement.

Mr. Bingley was smitten with Jane.

And Elizabeth knew that Jane was falling in love with Bingley.

Mr. Darcy was enraptured with Elizabeth and was growing more and more bewitched with her.

Elizabeth was beginning to wonder if perhaps he might be feeling such a thing.

That could not be! After all, he was Mr. Darcy of Pemberley, who would be expected to marry well.

And yet, she could not help but wonder.

Once more, Christmas Past brought the book forth, and the page turned again.

"Now here comes a Christmas that you especially enjoyed…"

CHAPTER 8

Christmas at Netherfield Park

D arcy and Christmas Past appeared at a window in the drawing room, which faced the lane in front of Netherfield Park. All around the place were Christmas decorations, and there were men and women, dressed beautifully, standing about, and talking.

There was a general merriment about everything, giving off every indication of being the wonderful time of the year.

"You know this event," Christmas Past said.

"Know it?" Darcy professed, with joy in his tone. "Of course I do. This was the Christmas Ball at Netherfield Park!"

Darcy looked around the room, saw his former self, waiting at the window for the Bennets to arrive.

"I couldn't wait to see them," Darcy said, explaining his younger self's thoughts. "Even though I knew that her younger sisters would be a little uncouth, and that her cousin would be a great nuisance." Darcy sniffed the air, annoyed. "That dreaded cousin Mr. Collins, came to see them, to make amends for being the one to inherit their entire estate. He meant well, but it does not change the fact that he is ridiculous."

"He wanted to marry one of the Bennet sisters, as an apology, did he not?"

"True. Whenever I would visit Longbourn, he would fawn over me, because I'm his patroness's nephew. Mr. Collins was as vexatious as Elizabeth warned me about. At first, she told me that he favored Jane, but their mama frightened him off from that. Then it was evident that he began to flirt with Elizabeth, but I would not have it. So, I would occupy all her company and kept him away from her. I believed that he understood, which is why he now tends to the next eldest, Mary. It would do well because they were a better match."

"They married eventually, did they not?"

"Yes, they did," Darcy said. "They still live at Longbourn. However, according to reports, Elizabeth could no longer bear Mr. Collins's constant subtle implications of being tired of supporting her as a burden."

"Yes, a bitter lesson, it is," the spirit acknowledged, "to be helpless."

"I suppose so."

Both Darcys saw the carriage roll down the lane, and the Bennets emerged, with their cousin, Mr. Collins, the reverend.

"There they are," Mr. Darcy uttered.

"There they are," his former self repeated, quietly.

Darcy looked at his former self, a little astonished. But then he realized that there was no way that one could be conscious of the other, and that it was just a coincidence that they said the same thing.

When Mr. Bennet and Mr. Collins helped the ladies down, they all began to walk up the steps.

Darcy's attention focused squarely on Elizabeth, who spied on his former self. When she and Jane were holding hands as they walked up the steps, Elizabeth investigated the window and smiled at younger Darcy.

He nodded to her, and walked away from the window, to meet her when she came.

Darcy followed his younger self, who stood behind the Bingleys as they greeted all their guests. Out of the side of his eye, he noted how Caroline Bingley had flashed an angry look at Elizabeth, and back at Darcy. There was no way that she was ignorant of the relationship that had grown between the two of them. Even though it is always illogical to be angry at someone who is liked by the person you feel a softness towards, it is still a common failing. Sadly, Caroline Bingley was still in the throes of that emotional ailment, and it would rest within her for a very long time.

For a moment, Darcy wondered if he had ever encouraged Miss Bingley or could have done something to help ween her off her affection—he found himself surprisingly feeling an ounce of sympathy.

In the next moment, his heart and head hardened again; in the end, what Caroline had ultimately done was self-inflicted. She would not recover from a path that she walked down and could have left eventually.

Even when she was to marry, a part of her soul was still on that path, which was most unfortunate.

Although these thoughts were interesting to explore, Darcy could not attend anything else, because his focus was solely on the woman who got away.

Darcy watched as Bingley and his family greeted everyone, including the Bennets. As Darcy's former self moved past Bingley, who was spending extra time talking to Jane, in the line of guests, he moved off to the side, catching Elizabeth's eye.

Once she was done thanking the host for having this ball, she moved out of the line and approached Darcy's former self.

"Well," she began, "welcome to an event that can either bring you pleasure or pain."

"Pain?" he asked, raising an eyebrow. "Are you going to attempt to hurt me?"

"Depends. Are you aiming to hurt me?"

"Not a jot."

"Then I shall not wound the Master of Pemberley. What would Derbyshire have to say if I were to do that?"

"Since I own a great deal of it, probably much."

"How large is Pemberley? You've made me curious, so I have the right to ask. And all this time that we've known each other, perhaps I should know the story behind the man who rides the length of Netherfield and points out that any savage can dance."

"Ten miles in diameter, approximately."

Elizabeth's eyes widened.

"Ten miles? Truly?"

"Indeed."

"Unless one is a king or queen, I marvel that someone

can have so much. It must be hard to maintain. Rewarding, yes, but I am sure that you rise to the occasion."

"I do my part."

Suddenly, Elizabeth pinched his arm. Naturally, this surprised him and put him back.

"Come now, man, I must have you help me on. This is a ball, I have done my best in the gown that a second daughter is given, and I can only continue a conversation for so long before I need help. I'm drowning, you know, and I need a bit of luggage to float on. A mere little will suffice."

"You are quite right," he allowed. "I wish I knew the right way to go about this, but alas, I know not."

"It's not your fault," she said. "I put you quite on the spot, and I do see that now. And there is the possibility that we now suffer from acquaintance-exhaustion."

He squinted, amusingly confused.

"What did you say?"

"It's a term that I've created: acquaintance-exhaustion. It's when you first meet someone, and when you begin to arrive at a better understanding, you tell them so many things. This can work well for the first five or six dinners with those two individuals, or the four dinners and two balls, or three balls and two tete e tetes. Take your pick of mixture. And then, after you've exhausted all conversation, you have nothing else to say. All you can do, therefore, is hope that a cow fell in the road, some natural disaster occurred, or someone in parliament suffered a scandal, so that you have something to talk about again."

"That's true," he acknowledged, "conversation is a well:

it's deep, nourishing, but eventually it can run dry. I do not want the well to run dry here."

"Nor do I."

"Let us return to pleasantries," he said, "and work our way forward from there." Younger Darcy offered Elizabeth his arm and they walk around the rest of the guests, wrapped up in their own world.

"I can support that notion," Elizabeth continued, "I look forward to the dancing."

"You love the activity."

"In the same manner that you dread it." She gave him a soft look. "Is there any chance that you have softened your outlook even more?"

"I am much less disposed to be against dancing a reel. Which puts me in the proper place to ask this question. Are you thus engaged for the first two dances?"

"Yes, I am," she replied.

Darcy watched his younger self feel forlorn.

"I am already dancing with you," she declared. "I already set you down as my partner, because I had the feeling that you would ask me."

He sighed.

"Miss Elizabeth, truly? You scared me for a moment. I thought that I would have to wait an entire hour before I could secure your hand."

"I could not help but tease you a little. You are the perfect target for my sharp words. You have the fortitude to take them. While I look forward to the amusement, there is only one problem with this plan."

"And what is that?"

"Well, since it's a Christmas Ball, naturally the evening

will end with the dance Sir Roger de Coverley. It's one of my favorite dances, but we cannot dance it together."

"Because dancing three times together would be too marked."

"Precisely."

"Oh, well. We shall find a way to endure."

He had a sudden revelation to be incredibly gallant.

"Miss Elizabeth, I forgot to mention something earlier."

"Yes?"

"You look lovely."

When hearing his compliment given so gently and so sincerely, it rendered Elizabeth speechless. Eventually, she had no choice but to find her voice again and thank him, which she did.

As the Christmas Netherfield Ball commenced, each Bennet sister had her perfect selection of a partner:

Jane was dancing with Mr. Bingley.

Elizabeth was dancing with Mr. Darcy.

Mary was dancing with Mr. Collins.

Kitty was dancing with Liam Lucas, the eldest son of Lucas Lodge.

Lydia was dancing with Sergeant Denny, who was one of the officers stationed in Meryton, under Colonel Forster's regiment.

Darcy walked up and down the dancers, at first, but since he was but a shadow, he realized that he could move in between them all and get closer to Elizabeth as she danced with his earlier self.

As younger Darcy and Elizabeth moved around the set, they passed Mr. Collins and Mary, who were having quite a delightful time.

"I never would have thought Miss Mary to be interested in dancing," Younger Darcy spoke, "she never did before."

"It turns out that she needed the proper inducement," Elizabeth said, "and our cousin proved to rouse her to desire the activity. It turns out, even though he is a clergyman, that he does not object to the amusement. Refreshing. I am happy for her. Despite that I find him ridiculous, he is the perfect sort of husband for Mary."

"I agree with you on all counts. She certainly is very pleased with him, and she shows it. They both look fondly at each other and do seem to be wholly inattentive to what goes on around them," he noticed as Mr. Collins almost bumped into another dancer as he was moving through the steps. He had been too focused on Mary to tend to much else.

"Oh dear," Elizabeth said, chuckling, "I fear that you are correct. A little too correct, sadly."

"Such a mistake can be forgiven," he accepted, "because of his focus on your sister."

"Precisely. I like how softly you gave that judgment. It was nicely done."

"It was so, because it's a little natural to become inattentive when you are with the person you care deeply for." He stared deeply into her eyes. "It's good to get lost into the spell that they place on you."

Elizabeth blushed and looked down, almost missing her own dance step in the process. He did his best not to notice.

"If Mary and Mr. Collins do not come out of this next

set less than enchanted with each other, I will be surprised," she pressed on, "yet, if they *do* then it shall prove my theory about dancing being a good incentive to two hearts coming together."

"Ah, you think of dancing as such?"

"Yes, I do. Some people find poetry to be the food of love, but I think it only works when the two people are in love already. But dancing! No, I believe that dancing is the best way of encouraging affection. See?" She nodded her head, gesturing to Jane and Mr. Bingley, who were dancing as well. "Dancing is the best ingredient to a mutual and affectionate alliance."

"For Bingley's part, perhaps," he responded, "but Miss Elizabeth, I still cannot help but not see enough regard in Jane's expressions toward him. The way that she looks at him is the same way that she looks at everyone. In her case, it would be pleasant to impose on the public and be less guarded."

"You still doubt me?" Elizabeth asked, not viciously, but imploringly. "Mr. Darcy, you really must believe me that Jane feels deeply for your friend."

"Very well."

"I can see that you are still not convinced. Never fear, we have time on our hands, and you might stumble on the idea that I am right, in this case."

"Do you ever believe that you are wrong?"

"When it comes to food and how to make coffee, yes, but with people, no." She smiled, Darcy's eyes softened, and they continued dancing.

"You never believed her though," Christmas Past said

to Darcy. "You never believed that Elizabeth was correct, and that Jane loved your friend."

"Miss Bennet never showed any particular regard for him," Darcy admitted. "Yes, she was always amicable, but never amorous. I admired Elizabeth, but I never believed her. I just could not."

"Another mistake," the spirit labeled.

"An observation," Darcy overrode.

As the ball proceeded nothing occurred to make it any less than a perfect evening.

Until the last dance occurred, which of course was Sir Roger de Coverley. When Mr. Bingley announced it, there was joy throughout the great hall.

When it was declared, Darcy's former self and Elizabeth were standing together, talking.

"And so begins the end of an enchanted evening," Elizabeth mused. "This dance is something that I shall not take away from you, for it cannot be made up for by conversation. Whom shall you dance with?"

Younger Darcy came to a decision.

"With you, if you will allow it."

Elizabeth's eyes widened and she blushed.

"With me?"

"Why ought we not to?" he questioned. "What rule must it be set down that we cannot dance a third time, innocently. Dance with me and be done with what others think."

Overjoyed, Elizabeth gave into the preferences for which she was beginning to feel for him. Much to her surprise, she was very much in the way of falling in love with him.

"Why not?" she realized. "There are some rules that are absurd. I do believe that this one is one of them. Let us break it and march on, to glory we go!"

They stood up and felt many people's eyes on them as they joined the other dancers, the musicians struck up the music, and they danced to steps to a popular reel done at Christmas.

As they did so, nothing could be more apparent:

Darcy had fallen in love with Elizabeth.

And it rendered her unable to do anything else but fall in love with him, in return.

"It was a Christmas ball the likes of which you ought not to have forgotten," Christmas Past said, "but you did forget, didn't you?"

"I chose *not* to remember," Darcy stated. "That was the correct course of action."

Christmas Past raised up the book.

"Come, my time grows short. Quick."

A page turned…

CHAPTER 9
The Turning Point

C hristmas Past and Darcy reappeared in a carriage that was driving through Kent.

They were sitting opposite Darcy's younger self. His face may be still and his manner grave, but in his eyes was an anxiety.

Recognizing the event easily, Darcy turned to the shadow.

"Spirit, why did you bring me here?" he asked. "Not now."

"These are but shadows of the things that have been. They are what they are, and that's what it shall be."

That was the only answer that he would be given. Sitting there, looking at himself when he was a few years younger, and still impressionable, he waited.

Eventually, they pulled onto Rosings Park, his aunt's estate.

Darcy and the spirit followed former Darcy into the great house, he was shown to his aunt's bedroom, and when he did, it was a harrowing sight.

His aunt, Lady Catherine de Bourgh, was lying in the bed, under the covers, with a doctor there to tend to her every need. His coming was well-meaning and correct, but ultimately fruitless, because the dowager was on the point of death.

Also standing against the wall was Mr. Collins, who was there to pray for her ladyship, and give her the last blessings and confession when a person must meet their maker.

Next to her bed, her daughter Anne was sitting in a chair, with Mrs. Jenkinson behind her.

Darcy nodded to them both, before he approached his aunt and sat down beside her.

Lady Catherine's eyes were closed; her breathing was raspy.

When Darcy was seated so close to her, he was humbled. Losing loved ones is an immortal tragedy. But what's more is to see someone that you were so accustomed to knowing as strong, determined, and a formidable force, now be reduced to a weak state—is hard.

If Lady Catherine de Bourgh had been born a man, or in an ancient culture where women did fight, she would have been a general, commanding armies against harsh lands, surviving it all. It was in her will power, and her way.

And now, to see her lying there, so brittle and so mortal, that it affected Darcy's heart.

"Aunt," Darcy's former self whispered, holding her hand. "Aunt Catherine…"

Her ladyship's head moved a little on her pillow, waking up slowly.

"Perhaps I ought not to disturb her," Darcy said to Anne and Mrs. Jenkinson.

"She would have wanted to hear from you," Mrs. Jenkinson said.

"I have performed all the correct rights befitting her ladyship," Mr. Collins said.

"Quiet!" Anne replied. This shushed Mr. Collins.

Darcy's former self felt Lady Catherine tighten her hand around his, indicating that she was waking up.

"Darcy," she uttered, her voice raspy and barely audible.

"Yes, aunt?" he stressed. "It's me. I'm here. I've come. I'm so sorry that I have been unable to come sooner."

"I…"

"Yes?"

"I need you… to do something for me." Her words were slow, and hard to utter.

"Anything," he assured her. "What is it?"

Her voice was so low that only he could hear it.

"I know that you do not love my daughter."

When hearing that, both Darcys blinked, astonished that their aunt would ever acknowledge such a thing.

With the younger Darcy, it was the first time he heard it.

But even with the present Darcy, hearing it again still amazed him.

"But still," Lady Catherine continued, "you can grow to. I know that you care for duty. Soon, I shall be dead."

"Don't speak like that. You may recover."

"I know it. I feel it. In time, I shall be dead. Anne will be the heir, and she will be defenseless. She will have no one to care for her but you. Do not leave her to be preyed upon by fortune hunters or marry someone who proved to be vicious. These things have happened. Do not let it occur to my daughter. You are the best thing for her. Please, do as your mother and I dreamed—do what you know is the right course to take. Do your duty. Save my daughter... from... the... world."

Her body spasmed, shook, and the doctor rushed to her, as Younger Darcy had to pry his hands from her.

Mrs. Jenkinson took Anne from the room, who was crying hysterically, and Darcy was also ordered to leave while the doctor tended to her, and Mr. Collins prayed.

By the end of the day, Lady Catherine de Bourgh had breathed her last and was now at peace.

The funeral was rightfully a dismal affair. Darcy's former self remained behind, to make sure that all burial arrangements had been properly made.

After Lady Catherine was placed under the ground, everyone went home.

Except Younger Darcy, who remained at her grave.

He stayed till the diggers finished placing the dirt over the coffin, and her ladyship was resting in her place.

While there, Darcy let his life flash before him, recalling his mother, all that she raised him to be. And for the duty that she had instilled in him.

To the greatness that his father bestowed on him.

To the sister who he had to maintain a level of respectability so that she could enter society with the highest of esteem.

To Bingley, who relied on him for sound and logical advice.

To his aunt, who believed till the end that her nephew would do right by her daughter.

To Anne de Bourgh, who needed a steady and firm hand, that was accustomed to running an estate.

To his late mother, who had so many dreams for him and who pleaded with him to remember what was owed to the greatness of family ties.

The weight of responsibility was felt so *heavily*, since it had been so *heavily* bestowed, that Darcy's former self was crushed under it.

"Aunt," Darcy's former self said to her grave, "you are correct, as my mother had been. My duty must be considered, and I shall not ignore all that has been given to me."

"That was the moment," Darcy said to the spirit, while watching his younger self, "where I conquered my heart, and strengthened myself against anything that did not align with the preservation of my family's respectability."

Eventually, the three of them returned to Rosings Park, and Mr. Collins was returning to Hunsford Parsonage. Before he took his leave, Mr. Collins informed Younger Darcy that he was going to write a letter to Longbourn.

"Since my dear Miss Mary Bennet and I might be on the way to achieving the proper sacrament of marriage, I am going to inform Longbourn of this sad business and how deeply your aunt's loss is felt. Is there any word that you wish to send to them?"

"Nothing," Darcy's former self responded.

"Nothing?" Mr. Collins was confused by this, but then

he had another thought. "Oh, you wish to speak to them about the event when you go into Hertfordshire again."

"I shall not be going to Hertfordshire ever again."

When hearing this, Mr. Collins's eyes widened in disbelief. This surprised him.

"But I thought that you…" Mr. Collins began, but his words were cut off when younger Darcy gave him a severe look.

"I shall not ever return to Hertfordshire," he repeated, "ever. And if you were to convey a message, inform Longbourn of such."

"I shall," Mr. Collins said, his voice weak from what that implied. Despite that Mr. Collins was not the cleverest of men, he still knew how to observe. Since he had seen how attentive Mr. Darcy had been to his cousin, Miss Elizabeth, he could not help but be a little alarmed. "Very well… very well."

Darcy's former self walked away from Collins, leaving the reverend in a disturbed state, as he went to dress for dinner.

In his customary guestroom that he had whenever he visited Rosings, his manservant, Jefferson, was taking out his change of clothes.

"Sir," Jefferson said, making sure that his master's waistcoat was suitable for the occasion, "If I may be so bold, I am so sorry again, for your loss. Lady Catherine was a wonderful aunt to you."

"Thank you, Jefferson. She was. I shall not forget the lessons that she has instilled in me."

"No proper nephew would do anything less. Also, for the sake of organizing all the proper arrangements—and forgive me for asking currently—but how long are we to remain here before we return to Hertfordshire?"

"We shall never be returning there."

"We are not returning to Hertfordshire?" Jefferson asked, surprised.

"No, we are not, Jefferson. I do not believe that I stuttered."

Hearing his stiff tones, Jefferson sensed that there was something irregular about his master's attitude. At first, he dismissed it, attributing it all down to Darcy's agony from losing his aunt.

"Forgive me, sir," Jefferson continued, "you spoke clearly. I was merely surprised."

"Ah."

"Do you wish to remain at Rosings for a longer time, or do you plan to go to London, since Mr. Bingley is currently there, on a matter of business?"

Younger Darcy considered that, came to another decision that would not only determine his own course of action, but Bingley's as well.

"That will do."

"Very good. I shall inform Mr. Hudson. He shall wish to know for how long you will remain in town before you go out to the country?"

"I shall remain in London, indefinitely, until I return back to Pemberley."

Mr. Jefferson blinked.

"There really shall be no return to Hertfordshire?" he asked.

"No return at all. And that is the final word on the matter."

Jefferson was no fool. He knew what his master was implying. He was abandoning his pursuit of Elizabeth Bennet and clearly was on the road to doing what he expected was his duty. Being the help, it was not his place to doubt, advise, or comment on his employer's actions.

But Jefferson had a way of connecting events to chains of thought. His master was throwing away his chance with Elizabeth Bennet, and was choosing to eventually marry his cousin, Anne.

Even though he could not predict the future, Jefferson felt the gravity of his master's actions. He knew that his employer was throwing away a woman he loved—and was at the beginning of him destroying his life.

Despite all these predictions and deductions, he was a manservant.

Thus, all that he could do was nod, agree and continue dressing his master for dinner.

Standing next to the Christmas Spirit, Darcy looked away from the scene.

Once more the spirit held out the book.

"Let us look at another Christmas Eve," she said, "that is not nearly as happy as the one that you left behind."

The scene shifted to another room in Rosings Park.

It was a parlor on the second floor, that was Anne de Bourgh's favorite room. It had been a year since Lady Catherine de Bourgh had passed away.

Darcy and the Ghost of Christmas Past appeared in the

doorway of the room, just in time to see a subtle, but still heated, debate.

Younger Darcy and Anne de Bourgh disagreed about their marriage.

Darcy was standing at the window, looking out of it, while Anne de Bourgh was seated by the fire.

"You do not wish to marry me?" Younger Darcy said, still looking out of the window.

"No, I do not," Anne de Bourgh responded. "I thank you for the compliment of asking me, and I apologize for causing any pain—yet I think that you do not feel any pain over this at all. After all, we do not love each other."

"Love?" Darcy turned around. "What does that matter, in this circumstance?"

"We do not have to marry, Darcy. There is no contract for why it should be so."

"I grant you that the engagement between us is of a peculiar kind. From our infancy we have been intended for each other. It was the favorite wish of my mother and yours. While in our cradles, they planned the union. And as we grew up, we understood that we were destined for each other."

"Yes, I have heard that wish many times over," Anne voiced, "but what is that to me? Or us for that matter?"

He turned to his cousin, astounded.

"How can you talk so? They were our mothers."

"Yes, they were. But they are *not* us. I loved my mother and my aunt, but their wishes are theirs. My life is mine. And I will not let anyone rule it."

"It is our duty!"

Anne de Bourgh stood up, gaining a surprising strength in her voice.

"Duty can go rot!" Anne hissed. "Darcy, we will not make each other happy. And I know that we have nothing to recommend us together. Yes, our mothers thought that I was not strong enough to run this estate myself, but I have done so, and I will continue to do so. And if I do marry, affection will be considered, if I choose to marry at all—which I confess, I am less inclined to marry."

Her cousin tensed, surprised by this reaction.

"You do not wish to marry?" he asked.

"Why should I?" Anne asked, shrugging her shoulders. "I have a large estate, am wealthy, and can run my life. I have full independence. Why would I want a husband to come in and take all that from me? Also, with marriage, comes children. I am thin and of a sickly constitution. I am not robust enough to survive motherhood. Having a child could easily lead to me dying, and I want to live as long as I can. I have family and will have some niece or nephew to tend to me, in some way."

As Anne walked around the room, she began to dream of all her plans that she had for the rest of her life.

"Now that I am my own mistress," Anne continued, "I can aspire to get well. I had dreams of visiting Matlock and Pemberley often. Maybe even being presented at court. And having all my family come here every Christmas. I wanted to maintain the tradition and make it all happier. I would even invite my tenants, and have many Christmas activities, and the children in the neighborhood put on a nativity play. Something to bring more life to Rosings Park. I have the perfect house to give annual balls.

I'm going to awaken this place, rather than let it be a mausoleum to my mother's intentions that would have hurt me."

All throughout her speech, Darcy felt betrayal weigh up in him.

At least, he translated it as such.

It was not betrayal. It was simply his good intentions being overturned by his cousin following her heart.

In a manner that he did not follow his.

It was disappointing.

"Anne!" he declared, "do be serious. And tell me that this sentiment will soon pass, and we shall do what is right."

Anne turned to him with a ferocity.

"I am doing what is right. You can come back tomorrow, or the day after, or the day after, but it will do no good. My answer will always be this. We shall not marry. I will never be content with 'enduring' my life. I have the right to live it in full."

"Cousin!" He struggled to breathe. He closed his eyes, embarrassed and heartbroken in knowing that his sacrifice came to nothing. Then he opened them again. "I have... made sacrifices so that I would do right by you. I have fallen madly in love with a woman, and then abandoned all pursuit in that direction, out of respect for you. I have turned away from my heart, and what she was easily growing to feel for me, for my promise."

"That is not my fault!" Anne said. "I am sorry that you have sacrificed so much on my account. But I never asked you to. In fact, if you had communicated this to me earlier, spoken to me, as cousin to cousin, I would have wished you joy and told you to choose her, whoever she might be. All of this could have been prevented if you had just communicated with me."

He rubbed his chin, losing all sense of stoicism as he felt his heart aching, under his own misconceptions.

"But you did not," Anne continued, "you were high-handed, made the decision for the both of us, and you hurt yourself in the process. I am sorry for you losing her. But you gain no ground by marrying me. Your sense of duty can now only lead to regret. I really am so sorry."

Bitter and filled with rage—though that rage had been directed in every other place but at himself, which was the only place for it to be directed—Darcy left the room, and quitted Rosings Park entirely.

"Did you ever speak to your cousin again?" Christmas Past asked Darcy.

At first, Darcy stood there, watching Anne de Bourgh sit back down in her chair. She was holding her head, from the ache that happens when you argue with someone passionately.

"No," Darcy answered, "I never spoke to her again."

"Like she said, it was not her fault."

"I know that now, but she followed her heart, and I didn't."

"And so, you could not forgive her for that."

"Don't say that."

"But it is true."

The Spirit raised up her book again.

The page turned…

CHAPTER 10
Closing the Book

W hen Darcy opened his eyes, he was at Bingley's house in London, in Grosvenor Square.

He and the Spirit were standing in the vestibule when there was a knock on the door. The butler opened it and Mr. Darcy's former self entered.

"No," Darcy cried when he saw the grave expression that his younger self bore. This memory also came to him quickly, and he did not wish to face it. "I do not need to relive this again to know what happened."

"But you will," the spirit uttered. "He deserves your memory of this, because you left it behind."

Darcy and the spirit followed his younger self into a parlor in the back of the house, where men usually break up after a dinner, to sit down and enjoy port and cigar.

When he was shown into the parlor, he found Bingley sitting down by the fire as the room's only source of light. After all, it was nighttime and the glow against Bingley's face was not a warm one, but a light that illuminated his anguish.

He was lying about the chair lazily, with a glass of brandy next to him, and a letter in his pocket.

"Bingley?" Darcy began.

"What brings you to Grosvenor Street?" Bingley asked, not looking at Darcy. "Let me see if I can guess. You have a dinner with a family of importance, and stopping off to see me along the way suited you."

"You could not be more inaccurate. I came to see you especially. Which you would know, because we had plans this evening. Plans which you have written to me, breaking them off."

"I sent word around in the proper amount of time."

"Yes. But it does not escape my notice that this is the fourth time that you have broken off any plans that we have made. Bingley, what is happening, man?"

"You are the great Darcy," Bingley said, "of profound intellect. Surely, you must know. For you know all."

"You are dangerously close to sounding vindictive for reasons that I am unaware of. I do not find pleasure in your tone."

Bingley chuckled sadly.

"She's courting someone."

"Who?"

Bingley raised up the letter.

"Miss Jane Bennet. Caroline wrote to me, informing me that she encountered Miss Bennet in a coffee house. She was with a gentleman, along with her sisters. Caroline had no choice but to greet them because they noticed her. Miss Bennet introduced the man, and Caroline learned that he and Jane were engaged in a courtship. According to Caroline, Jane looked exceedingly happy. Any man who would court her, but not marry her, is a great fool."

Bingley drank some more brandy.

Sensing that Bingley had heavily engaged in the cups, Darcy inspected the bottle and saw that it was half empty.

"You should not drink anymore."

"I do what I want!" Bingley cried. Putting down the cup, and the letter, he walked to the fire and began to stir it with the poker, to make it grow. "Because I spent too much time not doing what I wanted."

"What are you saying?"

"What I ought to have said before. I loved Miss Bennet, and I still do. I cannot help it. Now it's too late. When you and my sisters did everything to convince me that she did not love me—more and more, I believe that you all were wrong. Caroline and Louisa had motives of hoping that I would make a better match, especially regarding Miss Darcy."

"I suspected such," Darcy admitted, "I do not deny that my sister would have been a lovely choice for you."

"We do not love each other."

"I know," Darcy admitted, "that's why I abandoned the concept. I am aware that your sisters still cling to that wish."

"And you," Bingley uttered, "after your aunt died, you came back wholly changed. Something broke in you. I knew it when you would not return to Hertfordshire and gave Elizabeth Bennet up. I know that you were in love with her and then you forgot her. And so, where one house falls, so does the other. You prefer that sort of evenness; if you gave up on Elizabeth, then surely, I had to give up on Jane."

"That's not all that it was."

"Then what was it?"

"I truly believe that Miss Bennet was not in love with you."

"And I believe that you were wrong. I should have trusted my instincts, but I did not. You gave up one sister and I gave up the other, exposing us both to the world for caprice, and them to derision for disappointed hopes. And involving us all in misery of the acute kind. I blame you. But I also blame myself."

"In time, you will see that I was right."

Bingley looked at him, astounded and angry. In his friend's eye was a coldness that warmth should never spark again. In that moment, Bingley realized that he never knew his friend. It was like none of Bingley's words were reaching the master of Pemberley. As if there was a sliver of ice in his heart, which would not thaw. He felt like his friend was a stranger to him and Bingley had no wish to know him ever.

"I will never see it," Bingley said. "I always looked up to you and thought you right on all counts. Your experience and position in society has helped me. And your sureness of character, and strength, were all that I desired for a good friend who I could look up to like that of a brother."

Bingley turned to his friend.

"But because of my over-reliance on you, and lack of faith in myself, I am now in torment. I lost the love of my life, and I cannot forget that. You may find another upstart who idolizes you, to be their constant obedient friend. I will suffer this no longer. Our friendship is at an end."

"You have no right to say that," Younger Darcy declared. "I am the Master of Pemberley, of a great house."

Darcy's eyes turned even colder.

"You have no right to break off our friendship, due to my position and level in society that places me higher. I am your better. It is I that breaks off our friendship, which I am even more inclined to do."

Bingley chuckled.

"Even now, you feel nothing. I tell you that I no longer wish to be your friend, and there's hardly a reaction." Bingley tapped his hand against the table, resigned. "Just a cold eye? No attempt to reconcile. I should have known. Very well, since you are better, break off our bond. May your pride be contented now."

Younger Darcy barely reacted, and his voice was like stone.

"Our friendship is over, I take my leave of you, there will be a parting of the ways, and I have no wish to reunite it. Ever. Good evening, Bingley."

Darcy watched as his former self walked out of Bingley's townhouse, got into his carriage, and drove off.

Then he watched as Bingley sat back down, covered his face with his hand, and wept.

"That's how you ended a longtime friendship," Christmas Past noted. "With coldness."

"He chose to end it first," Darcy stated, "he brought it on himself."

"You really cannot see? You decided his fate because

you both could share the same misery. Very well, let us see one last memory."

Another page turned…

Darcy and the ghost appeared on Bond Street in London.

It was a day where the fog was most oppressive. The mist was neither uncustomary, nor unique, especially for that time of year.

Even though all the fireplaces in London were ablaze, they were fueled by coal, making the skies even heavier with fog. It was so overwhelming that when a person walked, they could not see another passerby until they were no more than two feet away from them.

Darcy moved back and forth through the smog, while the spirit stood there, with the vapors around her making it appear as if she was floating.

"Why have you brought me to this foul day?"

The ghost did not answer, and then Darcy realized what memory he had fallen into.

"This?" he said to the spirit. "You brought me here on this day?"

Christmas Past did not respond.

"Take me away," he said, "please?"

"Again, these are your memories," Christmas Past argued. "I did not create them. You did."

There were some people who passed Darcy on the street, appearing like spirits themselves, suddenly emerging from the fog.

At last, two figures were walking towards each other, wholly ignorant that they would meet.

Coming from one direction, was Elizabeth Bennet. From the other direction was Mr. Darcy's former self.

Because of the mist, Darcy did not see Elizabeth until she appeared right before him and moved through him. Feeling her essence, Darcy clutched his chest as he turned and saw his younger self come upon Elizabeth.

When colliding into each other, their astonishment was incredible, to say the least.

"Miss Bennet!" Younger Darcy exclaimed.

"Mr. Darcy!" Elizabeth said.

Both stood there, for a second, amazed that they had seen each other again, after it being a year since they had encountered the other.

The seconds turned into minutes.

At first, they remained there, staring at each other.

Both exchanged a sense of alarm, but on the man's side was mortification, and on the woman's side was a deep sense of indignation.

"I…" Darcy's former self began.

"I…" Elizabeth said, but then she recollected herself better than he did. Standing more erect, her full height giving weight to her words, she folded her hands in front of her, and continued speaking.

"Merry Christmas, sir," Elizabeth continued, "god save you."

"Yes," Darcy said, "though I am not quite fond of this time of year, thank you."

"You shall not offer me a Merry Christmas in return.

Come, Mr. Darcy, there is a set script for this time of the year."

"Like I said, I am not quite fond of the holiday."

"I don't see how you are less kind to this time than you are of any other time."

When hearing Elizabeth's pointed remarks, Darcy's former self was in a state of fascination and dread. To hear her speak was both agonizing for him but also intoxicating.

"I thought you were at Longbourn," he observed.

"And you have been everywhere, but Longbourn, for a year at least, therefore, I can understand you not knowing of my whereabouts. I am staying at my uncle and aunt's home, in Cheapside."

"The Gardiners."

"Yes. Despite that it has been a year since we have seen each other, I never had the ability to convey my condolences to you, for your aunt's passing."

"Thank you. And I am sorry for your parents passing as well. I know that must have been hard."

"Thank you. I never knew that you were aware of what we lost."

"Mr. Collins informed my cousin, Anne de Bourgh, of the matter when he left his position to become the new master of Longbourn."

He paused, awkwardly, before he continued.

"My cousin wrote to me of the matter. Again, I am sorry. Thus, you are staying at Gracechurch Street for the holidays and for a longer duration."

"While I found that I was not happiest at Longbourn any longer, my time in town is to gather a further acquaintance with another family."

"Ah, friends." Darcy's former self looked around, insecure, until he found something better to say. "What brings you out in this horrible fog on Christmas Eve?"

"The family that have invited me to stay with them has suffered an accident. The mother, a Mrs. Whitaker, has fallen ill, so I went to fetch the doctor."

"It was unsound of them to send a guest to fetch the apothecary."

Elizabeth wrapped her comforter tighter around her neck.

"You are very kind," Elizabeth overrode him, "but they are not being inconsiderate on their part, because soon they shall be my family."

Younger Darcy's eyes turned hollow.

"*Your* family?"

"Yes. Mrs. Whitaker will soon be my mother-in-law. For I am engaged to her son."

When hearing of Elizabeth being married to another man, it hurt both Darcys powerfully.

For the current Darcy, it was a second slice against his heart, because he had to hear it a second time.

"You are—engaged?" Younger Darcy asked.

"Yes. I am. Soon, I shall be a wife."

Darcy's former self looked away, staring into the fog.

Elizabeth had always been a creature of discretion and considering propriety when in public.

However, her curiosity, mingled with the offense that Darcy had inflicted on her when he removed himself from her society, made it altogether too difficult to be silent.

Having spent a year being unable to voice her feelings and frustrations to the man who she had considered giving her heart to, Elizabeth spoke her mind.

"What is that look for?" Elizabeth asked. "You cannot even find yourself to wish me well."

"I wish you well," he echoed.

"How hollow of you," she responded. "How like the calculating and careful man, using propriety to justify all manners of coldness and conceit."

"Miss Bennet—"

"I will suffer no false explanation that is used to quiet me," Elizabeth overrode, "it never worked before, so I am amazed that you would think it would work now. After you gave a terrible first impression when we met, I thought you changed. However, I was in error to have ever given you another chance. You returned to the man who I had chosen to despise beyond all others. And I was right. My only anger is that I changed my first perception of you."

Elizabeth saw how younger Darcy's face had not even moved. It was like he was stone. Elizabeth chuckled sadly.

"You were so close," she continued, "to feeling. To being something like human. You were growing to love me. It is not vanity to say so, but fact. As I was falling in love with you. As Jane and Bingley were falling in love with each other. You came so close to exposing your heart to something that was real. But you did what I should have suspected. You abandoned all hopes in the shades of Longbourn and left me behind. I know how you convinced Bingley to abandon Jane. There's no point in arguing because I made the connection. One moment, Bingley is with us, happy with Jane, then he goes to London, where you meet him there, and he never returns. Do you deny it?"

"I have no wish to deny it. I did everything to separate Bingley from your sister. And I was right. You both have now been made penniless from the death of both your parents."

Elizabeth felt the offense that she had every right to feel. But it would not break her.

"I regret the day that you came to Hertfordshire."

"I did love you," Darcy admitted.

"But that was not enough, was it?" Elizabeth said.

"I had my duty."

"And I have mine. A duty to my self-respect. You closed the door on whatever we had. Now I close this discussion on you. I am not beneath you—you are the one beneath me. You were never worth a thing. The great idol of your 'duty' has displaced me in your heart, so I am not enough for you. You may—the memory of what is past half makes me hope you will—have pain in this. But it shall be a very, very brief time, and you will dismiss the recollection of it, gladly, as an unprofitable dream, from which it happened well that you awoke. I will not wish you to be happy in the life you have chosen. Because look at you; you doomed yourself to misery. Goodbye."

Turning away, she walked through the fog and disappeared.

Darcy took a few steps, shouting after her.

"Don't go!" he cried to her retreating form. "I did love you. I never stopped!"

Darcy turned back to his younger self, who remained in the fog, his face cold and indifferent.

"You fool!" he yelled at his younger self. "All you ever did was make every mistake!" Once more, he realized that he was shouting at himself. "What a fool I was."

His younger self faded away into the mist and dissolved.

All that was left, in the dense London fog, was Darcy and Christmas Past.

"Spirit," Darcy said, in a broken voice, "remove me from this place."

"Do you feel that word yet?" Past asked him. "Regret?"

"Remove me. I cannot bear it!"

Christmas Past raised up her arm and pointed behind Darcy.

Through the fog, Bingley's form appeared.

In another spot, Anne de Bourgh materialized.

Through another place in the fog, Caroline Bingley emerged.

To the left, from out of the denseness, Jane Bennet appeared.

To the right, Georgiana appeared.

Then, through the most intense part of the fog, Elizabeth's figure emerged.

They all seemed to swarm around Darcy, forcing him to confront the darker parts of himself that he would not relinquish.

He felt their eyes on him.

The main gaze that made his knees weaken was Elizabeth's as her sparkling eyes somehow penetrated the fog's dreary aspect and he felt pain under it.

Shutting his eyes, he turned back to Christmas Past.

"Leave me!" he cried. With an impulse, he grabbed the book that held all his memories. "Take me back! Haunt me no longer!"

He threw the book high in the air and far away from him. It disappeared into the London mist.

When it was gone, the fog swiveled around him, Darcy roared out, as he felt like his body was being whipped about by a great force.

Christmas Past disappeared, as did everything else around him, when he found himself collapsing in the chair in his sitting room, by the fire.

An extreme exhaustion overcame him, and beyond his control, he fell asleep.

CHAPTER 11
The Second of the Three Spirits

Awaking in the middle of a prodigiously heavy slumber, Darcy was met with darkness.

Suddenly, an incredible light protruded from the pianoforte, along with a beautiful melody.

The light reached such a pitch that Darcy had to shield his eyes.

"Stand up, man!" cried a powerful, but congenial voice. "Hear what you must hear. And see what is brought forth to you."

"How can I see when the light is so blinding?" Darcy asked, shutting his eyes, as he attempted to stand up.

"The brightness harms you?" she asked.

"Yes, it does."

"Very well. I shall diminish the scene, but I refuse to dim the light that I give."

The ghost lessened the illumination and at last, Darcy was able to open his eyes.

When he did, he was amazed.

The walls to his room had been almost entirely done

away, and he was amidst a winter wonderland with snow, icicles and a beautiful woodland sweeping out before him.

His furniture was still there, but the scene shifted from being his sitting room to the left, to being the lovely Christmas scene to the right.

Music played from the pianoforte, but there was an even more incredible sight.

On top of the instrument, was a beautiful arrangement of holly, pinecones, berries, snow and other indicatives of the Christmas season.

Above all that was a throne made up of the foundations of a tree that stretched up far and beyond sight, wherein a woman sat atop it, wearing a beautiful modern gown, with a sweeping train at the back which ran the length of the room.

In her hand, was some sheet music.

"Come closer!" she cried, "and know me better, man!"

Darcy stood up, timidly. Since encountering the first spirit, he was prepared for almost anything. As such, he did not meet this ghost with shock, but simple wariness.

The closer he got; he inspected the spirit's face. Though her eyes were clear and kind, he had a hard time staring into them.

"You are the second ghost who I was told that would come," Darcy asserted.

"Yes. I am the Ghost of Christmas Present."

Darcy looked at the floor.

"Look upon me!"

When Darcy did so, he marveled at her appearance. Though she was wearing the current fashions belonging to present times, there was still something otherworldly about her.

"You have seen the likes of me before," she said, "but never in this manner, have you?"

"No," he said, "not in this manner."

"I suspected as such. You bear the fortune, Fitzwilliam Darcy of Pemberley, Derbyshire, to glimpse the spirit of Christmastime, and then to walk alongside it."

"I expect so. I do not suppose that this night will end until I have allowed you to take me where you will."

"It is a delight to see that you possess some intelligence," Christmas Present said, beginning to laugh heartily. "If you want to see the end of this adventure, there is no going back—forward. Only forward."

"Then conduct me where you will. But I must ask you not to force me to relive the hard agonies of my history."

"Recall my name," she uttered, "I am not the past, but the present. But time shall make you understand how this all is entirely for the good of your side."

"I went forth before on a compulsion," he said, "but now with a better understanding. Lead on."

Christmas Present lowered her throne, to the point where she was standing on top of the piano.

She opened the sheet music and placed it in front of Darcy.

"Touch the many notes of music on the page."

"Why so?"

Christmas Present laughed merrily.

"You shall see."

As soon as Darcy had touched the music selection, a large assortment of bells began to play beautifully.

Darcy saw that he and Christmas Present shrunk to a small size and disappeared inside of the pianoforte.

Feeling the sensation of being yanked in different directions, he held onto Christmas Present for dear life.

"Spirit!" he roared, "what is happening?"

"Life is compiled of sounds," Christmas Present answered, "and we hear them as soon as they are born. We all have an instrument that plays the tune to our lives, and the melody that changes as time wears on. Yet, I doubt that you ever took time to listen."

Since they had shrunk in size, they moved through all the many internal parts of the pianoforte, from the sound-board to the rim, the lock rail, and eventually they began to slide along the strings.

Knowing that he was on the inside of the very instrument that his mother and sister played fascinated him.

As they sped along the strings, it morphed into a street in London, from Kennington Lane to Wimpole Street. Yet 'sped' was not the correct word for it. Rather, they were flying through the streets, where there were children and families singing Christmas carols, hoping to get a penny or anything from passersby.

There were butchers and bakers who were letting people cook their Christmas dinners in their ovens, as well as children playing in the streets, sliding down the sheets of ice, and having snowball fights.

All while they flew, Darcy was able to hear the songs that each person seemed to give off. Their own habits and ways of being had their own melody.

"Do you hear it all?" Christmas Present pointed out. "All these sheets of music that come with daily life."

"Yes," Darcy admitted, amazed, "I do hear it. I hear it all. How could I never have noticed until now, that life has its own tune?"

"Because you never cared to hear it."

Darcy didn't answer, wondering if perhaps the spirit had been correct. Had he not heard the tune of life before? It was a rush of different instruments, playing slow and quicker tempos that all seemed to rush together in a way that flowed organically.

Darcy let the tune wash over him and it was not like he was seeing the objects of beauty that adorned the holiday season and felt the magnitude of it through hearing.

He heard the holly, mistletoe, red berries, ivy, turkey, geese, game, pudding, fruit, and punch that filled many dining tables on that special day.

Despite that London was so bleak, especially since the sky was gloomy, and the shortest streets were choked up with a dingy mist, and half-frozen under the snowfall, there was still an air of cheerfulness about everything.

There were many people on the streets, buying food from the poulterer's shop, which was half-open. The fruit shops always had someone in them.

"Let us see London, from a higher view, and the music that makes it move."

Darcy and the spirit flew higher, along the music of the night, over houses, where people were shoveling away on their rooftops, seeing many people moving about their homes through the windows, all singing merry songs, playing games, exchanging gifts, being called away to church, or at parties.

Darcy's eyes widened in amazement and—dare he

think it—happiness as he flew over the city and saw it from a height that few mortals had the ability to witness.

They flew over many streets, areas from Paddington to the Borough, passed St. James Palace, Big Ben, over Christ Church, London Bridge, the Thames River, where Darcy was able to see a great deal of Central London along the melody of the atmosphere.

"It's beautiful!" Darcy acknowledged, "and it—"

He was speechless when all the roads began to form distorted lines that eventually straightened out, as the buildings all turned into notes, and London became a long string of music on a page, while still thriving and alive.

"It's…" Darcy trailed off.

"Every city is a song," Christmas Past said, "because every song is a story. Sometimes the story is beautiful, other times, it's ugly. It can be joyous. It can be sad. It can be heroic, or villainous. But never silent. Never gone. But on this day, what it always ought to be: merry."

They flew through the London Skyway and landed on a small road near Tooley Street, in the Borough.

They landed right in front of a modestly-sized house, that was kept up as best as could be to a family that was constantly at work.

"Spirit," Darcy said, looking around the area, "why do you bring me here? I have nothing to do with this area of town."

"You don't, but your butler does."

"Mr. Hudson?" Darcy raised an eyebrow. "This is where his family lives?"

"Yes. His mother lives here, with his sisters, brother-in-law, and his nieces."

"I never knew that Hudson had that much family."

"He's a servant; he's not supposed to have any that you would care to hear of, I believe."

"It is not required of a master to know his servants' familial lives."

"True it is not." Christmas Present leaned into Darcy, her eyes growing intense, and intimidating. Though she did not look vicious, he felt the full meaning of her intentions and it humbled Darcy.

"But that does not mean that you must give into that custom, now do you? You were about to not even give them a Christmas, when you could have. Just because you are told that someone is lesser than you, does not mean that you must believe it!"

Darcy found himself intimidated under her gaze.

"Because that's what led you down the path where you lost much," Christmas Present added.

Next, her eyes shifted from menacing to kind again.

"So, until I have finished my work on you," she concluded, "we will be continuously in argument. It is never wrong to know the lives of those around you."

Christmas Present smiled suddenly.

"And speaking of the man himself, soon your butler shall arrive. Therefore, shall we go in?"

"Into his family's home?" Darcy asked, finding this part of the journey needless.

"Maybe you might see something that you need to see."

"What?"

"A happy family. Something you once belonged to."

Seeing that it was useless to argue with the ghost, Darcy

yielded and as they moved through the door, they entered a house full of activity.

While the dwelling was humble, it was still clean overall. There was some dust in corners, but that was natural when there is a family of that size.

Moving back and forth were two women who looked alike. They were preparing the meal, from making the pudding to mushroom dressing and the potatoes.

A girl around the age of fourteen was putting the finishing touches on the mincemeat pie.

"Well then," Darcy asked, "who is who?"

"Those are Mr. Hudson's sisters, Elinor and Marianne," Christmas Past explained. "Elinor is the married sister, to a Mr. Edward Pennyworth, and they have four daughters. The girl is Mr. Hudson's niece, Belinda. She's the third sister of the four. The eldest daughters are Belle and Fan. They are currently employed in factories and are trying to get home for Christmas dinner. The youngest daughter, Martha, is at the bakery with her father."

"Is Uncle John coming for Christmas?" Belinda asked.

"Oh, he better had be," Marianne said, "Mama would be heartbroken. And if he does not ask that ornery master of his to let him have Christmas off, I have half a mind to walk up to Mayfair and start a scene."

"Marianne," Elinor chided her, "you wouldn't dare."

"I would, Elinor," Marianne said, checking the potatoes. "I just need our brother to give me his permission."

"You'll lead to John losing his position if you do that. Be reasonable."

"I'm always reasonable. Just not in matters such as this. And what about Belle?" She asked Elinor and Belinda.

"Where is she? She's usually not this late in coming. The factory could not be open today, surely."

"It shouldn't be," Elinor said, "but sadly, their master is just as much a thwarter to Christmas plans as John's employer. He always finds a way to get some of the women in his factory to fetch errands for him to help with his Christmas dinner party. But Belle assured me that she would come. I hope so. I would not be as happy with this day not having all my daughters here."

Belinda looked out of the window.

"Father, Fan and Martha are coming," Belinda exclaimed, "and they've got the goose with them and the wine and punch!"

"Wine?" Elinor asked, rolling her eyes. "Oh, your father!"

Belinda yanked the front door open, and her father, Edward, entered, carrying the wine and punch, with Fan carrying the goose, and little Martha, who was seven years old, was carrying some fruit.

"The bakery smelled brilliant when we got the goose done," Martha shouted. "It smelled like... oh, I cannot explain it. Fan, what did it smell like?"

Fan, a delicate but happy girl of eighteen, decided to help her sister.

"Sage, onion, and every good thing."

"A better goose could not be found," Edward said, "well, not a better goose for twelve pence, that is."

"Twelve pence will do for the family," Elinor said, kissing Edward on the cheek as Edward spun her around. Then she gestured to the wine. "But that, I'm not so certain."

Edward picked up the wine.

"My dear," Edward said, "it's Christmas."

'I know it's Christmas, but I also know that you wanted to save up so that you could buy yourself a new waistcoat and boots. This will keep you from that."

"Sometimes you have to enjoy life, even when it's not sensible."

Elinor made a face at him.

"You brought the wine because you know that I like wine, didn't you?" she asked.

Edward looked guilty.

"No," he said.

"Yes," Elinor overrode him. "My love, I don't want you to lose your savings for my happiness."

"What is a husband who does not spoil his wife every now and then?"

Elinor couldn't help but smile.

"I have no choice but to be overjoyed, don't I?"

"Precisely," Edward said, holding mistletoe over their heads.

Laughing, they kissed.

Marianne and her nieces both made a face at each other, chuckled, and went back to preparing the meal.

"Are you nauseated from watching their happiness?" Christmas Present asked Darcy.

"You are presuming to know what's in my mind," Darcy said.

"Are you telling me that I am wrong? I bid you luck in trying to lie, sir. Or does your unease stem from something more painful?"

Darcy ignored the question by deflecting.

"Please," he said, "I am trying to hear."

"Oh!" Marianne said, looking out of the window, "no need to worry about Belle being late."

"You see her?" Edward asked, "good."

"She's coming down the road with John."

"Wonderful," Elinor said, and she turned to her youngest daughter. "Martha, go and tell your grandmother that John is coming."

"Yes, Mama," Martha responded, going upstairs to wake Grandmother Hudson up.

Once more, the door opened again, and Darcy watched as Mr. Hudson entered, carrying some bags, and linking arms with a handsome young woman, who must've been his eldest niece, Belle.

~

"Brother!" Marianne exclaimed. "Finally, you make your way back to us." Rushing to her brother, she embraced him and Belle.

"Merry Christmas, Marianne," Mr. Hudson responded, laughing as she almost made him fall over. "You know that I always find my way back home."

"I know, I know, I know."

"I was worried about neither of you coming," Elinor said to them both as Edward hugged their eldest daughter, and Elinor also hugged her brother. "Why bless your heart, my dears, how late you are."

"It was neither of our fault," Belle responded. "Uncle Hudson can explain his side, and my employer, once again, made us help him prepare for his Christmas party tonight.

At least I got a shilling by way of it. That led to me being able to get chestnuts so that we could roast them."

"Fine addition to the dinner," Edward said, "I am glad you are come, my dear. And merry Christmas, John."

"Merry Christmas as well," Mr. Hudson said, clapping his brother-in-law on the shoulder.

Mr. Hudson looked around, still amazed that he was able to attend.

"I still regard my coming as a miracle," he continued, "but I see that you got my letter by express that I was going to be here. I had to make sure that Master Darcy had everything he needed before I was able to come away. Poor Jefferson must remain behind, though. But he was kind enough to give me this, since he had no family, he knew that I had much."

He looked at Elinor and Marianne.

"Sisters," Hudson continued, "I am certain that this is going to be the best meal ever."

"Oh, I do hope so," Elinor said, "I managed not to burn anything this time."

Laughing he kissed his sisters on the cheek.

"How is Mama?" He asked. When not seeing her, he was worried and assumed the worst. "She is not—"

"She is well," Elinor assured him. "She is resting upstairs and must always keep to her room now."

"I know," he replied, his eyes downcast. "I just wish…"

"I know," she said, finishing his thought. Both looked at each other, understanding the other, as brother and sister often do.

Behind him, Marianne pulled the potatoes from the fire.

"What excellently boiled potatoes," Hudson said, chuckling.

"Are you about to mock me because potatoes are the only thing that I know how to cook well?"

"Let me tease my beautiful sister a little bit. And still, I cannot understand why you are not married. I have served some of the best the London ton has to offer, and many of them are not half so handsome as you."

"You know me," Marianne said. "When it comes to choosing a man, I require so much."

"Very well, and perhaps you ought to. The only reason I was happy that Elinor married was because Edward was worthy of her."

"Oh," Edward said, warming himself by the fire. "That's what it was?"

"Yes."

Edward chuckled.

"I am happy to know that you still like me. And Belle, warm yourself by the fire, dear. I don't want you to catch cold."

Belle obeyed.

"And how came you both to arrive together?" Edward asked Mr. Hudson. "It was timely met, I see."

"We met on the omnibus," Belle said, warming her hands over the flames. "When I got on, Uncle Hudson was there. He told me stories of everything that he has done at the Darcy house since this summer."

"Which wasn't much, sadly," Mr. Hudson said, "since my master is not fond of society."

"We know!" Everyone said in unison.

For Christmas Present, it was comical.

For Mr. Darcy, it was a little disconcerting that they all seemed aware that he lacked much social connection.

"And where is little Martha?" Hudson asked.

"Oh, she's—," Elinor began, but she was cut off by her youngest daughter coming downstairs, having heard her uncle.

"I'm here, Uncle Hudson," Martha cried, running up to him. She jumped into his arms, and he twirled her around.

"I was just waking grandmother."

"There's a good girl," he said. "Now, line up you four, so that your prodigal uncle can look at you all."

From oldest to youngest, the four of them lined up from Belle to Fan, Belinda, and Martha.

"I have grown an inch since we last saw each other," Belinda said, "Mother and Father said so."

"And their authority is the best to go on!" he said, looking at them, with pride. "You four are quite the women, I believe. There aren't four prettier sisters in the whole of London, I daresay."

"Oh," Fan said, blushing. "I am getting better at receiving compliments. I really am."

"Still modest."

"We worried you would not come for Christmas, so imagine when we got your letter. And now we are to be together all the Christmas long and have the merriest time in all the world."

Hudson smiled.

"You are quite the woman, little Fan. Now I should see Mother."

Mr. Hudson went upstairs.

"A mother and son reuniting," Christmas Present said. "Nothing more wonderful than that, wouldn't you agree?"

Having no choice but to make the connection, Darcy recalled the feeling of seeing his mother again, even as a ghost.

"Yes," Darcy responded, "that is a true philosophy."

From outside of the house, there were some carolers singing 'Hark the Harold Angels Sing'. The music raised Darcy and the spirit up, who flew into Mrs. Hudson's room.

It was small, the air was stuffy, but it was warm and cluttered from all the items that Hudson's mother had collected through the years that usually comforts an invalid, when they cannot go to the world in the manner that they were accustomed to.

In the bed was Mrs. Hudson, who was in her late eighties.

"Hudson's mother," Darcy uttered.

"Yes," Christmas Present confirmed. "Decades of harsh and arduous work has worn on her, while raising three children, after their father died. She swore no matter what that she would never let her children starve or take them to the workhouses. For her to have made it to her eighties is remarkable. Mothers have a habit of finding a way, do they not?"

"Yes."

Mr. Hudson appeared in the doorway. When seeing his mother in bed, he motioned for her to stay as she was and not try to rise. Either way, it did not affect the joy in seeing her son again.

"Mother," Mr. Hudson said, moving through Darcy, actively walked towards his mother's bedside, bent down, and took her hands in his. "I've come home for Christmas."

"I never thought you would," Mrs. Hudson said. "I have wanted you to for these last four years."

"I know," her son responded. "I am sorry."

"I know that it was not your fault. I was happy to see you in August, but you had to leave so soon."

"I have my… duties. But I'm here now, and when I was able to take the day off, the first thing in my mind was to go home directly. I've come home for Christmas with my family. With you."

Mr. Hudson's eyes were misty.

"How fortunate we all are, Mother," he continued, "to still have you with us."

His mother shook her head.

"I feel like such a burden."

"Nonsense," he responded passionately. "All your life you looked after us. A woman who suffered as much as you would have broken, but you didn't. You kept going and therein giving us what we are at present. And now we can have a future."

"My dear good boy," Mrs. Hudson said, running her hand gently down his cheek, "I… when I was younger, I told myself that I would never be weak. That I would always be strong to the very end. But life broke me, as it has done to many of us when we live longer than we ought. I never wanted to be a burden to you all, so."

"Mother, please," Hudson stressed. She had often

spoken to him that way before, but he dismissed it as a mood that would soon pass. Looking at her, he wanted her to believe every word that he said. "Live. Live to be a hundred. Live to see so much more and be there for us. You gave all your strength to us. Just for the sake of it, for Christmas, let us always be strong for you. Now, come."

Hudson lifted the blankets that covered her, he wrapped her shawl over her shoulders, picked her up and carried her downstairs.

When he did, the dinner was prepared.

They all rushed to help the matriarch of the family sit down at the head of the table. Seeing her family care for her, Mrs. Hudson felt so moved that she almost wept.

When they laid out the food, Mrs. Hudson offered up the prayer. As she ended it, she looked around.

"I have all my children and grandchildren here," she said, "the greatest gift in the world. Even the king and queen are nowhere near as fortunate as I."

Happy was the entire meal given. Yet, despite the size of the family, the meal was not very much. But no one complained.

At last, the dinner was done, the cloth was cleared, the hearth swept, and the fire made up. Apple and oranges were placed on the table, and a shovel full of chestnuts on the fire.

All the family drew round the hearth.

Edward poured everyone a cupful of wine, and it came time for the round of toasts.

Each person gave thanks and appreciation for their family, and then thanks to something small. No matter how insignificant. Once someone toasted, you took a small sip, so that there would be enough in their cups for everyone's toast.

When it was Mr. Hudson's turn, he raised his cup.

"To my family, which I am truly blessed to have in my life. And to my master, Mr. Darcy, who was kind enough to give me a day off so that I could be here with you now."

When hearing his name mentioned, Darcy was flabbergasted.

On such a day for his butler to remember him brought a warm feeling to himself. After all, no one could be so cold that they couldn't feel the depth of the compliment.

Unfortunately, the warm feeling was not shared by anyone else other than himself.

After all, Hudson knew him, but not the family. As such, they had no loyalty to him.

Everyone looked at each other, displeased with the latter part of the acknowledgement, but Marianne was the first to drop her cup.

"Kind indeed!" Marianne groaned. "I wish that he were here, so that I could give him a lecture of how far his kindness stretches."

"Marianne," Mr. Hudson responded. "It's Christmas Day."

"She's right to be angry," their mother added, "it ought to be Christmas, I am sure, on which one drinks the health of such a cold, inconsiderate, hard, and unfeeling man as Mr. Darcy."

"Uncle Hudson," Belle added, "consider, this is the first Christmas that you have shared with us in four years."

"And we barely see you for the rest of the year, but maybe three times," Fan added. "I am friends with many servants in grand houses, and they are given more days off than you. Even butlers. And they never go more than two years without being given a Christmas holiday."

"Aunt Marianne is right to be mad," Belinda uttered.

"Here, here!" Martha added, because that was all that she could think of.

"You must not be angry with your nieces," Mrs. Hudson uttered, "they just miss you, and because of Mr. Darcy, they barely know their uncle."

"While the wealthy will have their whims and ways," Elinor added, "and always prefer to have things always to their liking, you are a talented butler. Can you not find another family to work under, who is less strict in their requirements?"

Mr. Hudson looked around the table and felt elated, knowing that they missed him.

As a result, he realized that he owed his family some explanation for why he remained loyal to Darcy throughout all these years.

"In my line of work," Mr. Hudson began, "it is never right to judge or speak of our betters, which includes our employers."

Hudson put down his cup, and breathed in heavily, about to break his cardinal rule.

"Nor is it right to talk of what happens with the family that we serve, to anyone outside of the house. But there is something about my employer that you need to be aware of."

He looked around the circle of his family and attempted to explain, without giving away too much.

"Mr. Darcy was different once," Hudson continued, "he was a man who was raised with specific obligations that, for all his wealth, was very confining. Then something occurred where he could have deviated from what was expected of him and did something that might have made him continue to be a better man. There was a time where he was happy, and we felt his happiness enhance his treatment toward us. But then he made a choice against his better judgment. And that choice broke him."

The firelight brought more illumination to Hudson's kind features.

"While it is always best to not allow your happiness to rely on external forces—and by that, I mean that our goodness should always be dependent on our own morality and internal willpower. Rather than needing some other outlet to create our better natures. It is not sound. Or wise. But we are all human. And sometimes, we cannot always lean toward logic and give way to it. Our disappointments and failures can get the best of us."

"But Mr. Darcy has everything that he could want," Fan said, "and has so many resources."

"All, but one," Hudson continued, "while he never mentioned it to me, we servants can overhear many things and then the incident can spread to the rest of us. Rumor is a powerful thing, especially in a household. Something occurred which would have guaranteed my master's happiness. Everything about it would have made his life, and ours better."

Hudson took a sip of wine.

"Sometimes, we're on a path, then we reach a fork in the road, and we can turn left, right, or stay going straight. Darcy should have taken a left. It would have been the making of him. But sadly, he kept going straight. He did what he was trained to call his duty. Then, after he made that choice, that sacrifice, it was all for nothing. Mr. Darcy not only suffered a mass disappointment, but he was humiliated. And so, he never recovered. And he continued to fall, until us servants is all that he has left. That's why I cannot hate him. All I can do, despite all his wealth, is feel sorry for him."

When he finished, Edward leaned forward.

"Well," Edward added, "with that considered, we'll drink his health for your sake, and for the day's. To Mr. Darcy."

"Yes," Elinor said, "to Mr. Darcy."

Marianne would never fully feel pity for him, but they all drank to Mr. Darcy's good fortune.

When hearing the truth presented so simply and so blatantly, Darcy couldn't stand it any longer.

He rushed out of the house and stopped in the middle of the street.

Bending over, he felt grief swell up in him, unable to run from the truth any longer.

He wanted to marry Elizabeth Bennet.

Then he abandoned her.

He chose to marry Anne de Bourgh instead.

And she refused him.

As he remained there, shaking, he heard Christmas Present appear behind him.

"He understands you," the spirit said, "you have a great butler."

"Yes, I suppose that he is," Darcy admitted. "I never knew that he was such a person."

"He's right, isn't he?" Christmas Present asked, standing next to Darcy.

It was heavy to admit, but there was no point. He could not lie to the ghost, because she would know that he was being deceptive.

"Yes," Darcy nodded. "It was all for nothing. Sacrificing my heart was *all for nothing*. And I had to live with knowing the love of my life despises me, and it ruined my relationship with my cousin. After that, what was the point of anything?"

"There's always a point to many things."

Christmas Present raised up the sheet of music.

"Come. We have more to see."

Darcy and the shade disappeared along the music lines and notes of life on Christmas Day...

CHAPTER 12

Berries & Holy

Wthen they appeared again, it was at Bingley's townhouse.

"Grosvenor Square," Darcy deduced. "Spirit, why bring me here? I could find nothing by seeing how Bingley spends Christmas. He probably will not even want to hear my name mentioned."

"Because it was at Christmastime that the Netherfield Ball took place."

"Yes."

"Well, this is the moment for you to understand that it's not always about you. Rather, sometimes it's about someone else, and your effect on them."

They entered the establishment, where there was a party of many people who were dressed wonderfully.

The party served two functions: it being a Christmas party, and an engagement party for Caroline Bingley.

Even though his personal life had not turned out the way that he liked, Bingley was not the sort to let it kill his soul and cheerful manner.

He still was determined to be open and amicable to everyone he met.

But internally, a part of himself was shattered.

While everyone was talking, Mr. Bingley stood up and tapped his glass.

"Being a dinner party, especially at Christmas," Bingley began, "a toast is one of those rituals that it seems to be awful to not do."

All the guests chuckled.

"And so, I am happy to be able to give two toasts. To everyone here, I wish you all a merry Christmas, and a happy new year. But for the most treasured of announcements, I take pleasure in what a brother ought to."

He turned to Caroline, and her fiancé was seated right next to her.

"Caroline, I wondered if you would ever find a man worthy of you. Therefore, I take pleasure in knowing that you found him."

Caroline took her fiancé's hand, who smiled down at her.

"Nothing about this alliance is anything else but a joyous occasion, and you both understand each other, and adore each other. That's all that one can hope for when they find the love of their lives."

Suddenly, Bingley faltered. All over his face, memories came back to haunt him.

Darcy recognized this affliction, and what sparked it.

As soon as the heartbreak began to materialize, Mrs. Hurst and Caroline saw it and exchanged an apprehensive look.

Since she was older and more accustomed to standing

by her brother, Mrs. Hurst decided to save her little brother.

"Oh, Charles!" Mrs. Hurst declared. "You are so over-powered by the good news, that it almost made you fall down!"

The guests laughed.

This was enough to bring Bingley back to the present. His smile returned to its customary place, and he continued with his toast.

"At this merry time of year, the greatest gift is finding the happiness of loving and being loved in turn. You have found it, and I wish you all the joy in two becoming one. To my sister and future brother-in-law!"

The toast was given, and they all drank.

"Now!" Caroline's fiancé said, "where is the mistletoe? I have a great desire to kiss my future wife."

Everyone laughed.

"Well," Caroline said, "I think I have one stored in my petticoat somewhere!"

They all laughed again.

"She does love him," Darcy said to the ghost.

"She does, almost in the way that she preferred you," the ghost augmented, "never fear of feeling like you failed her too much. She had room to fall in love with someone else, and she did. Her pride is merely hurt from your choices, but she will recover."

"I ignored her feelings for me, you understand," Darcy said. "That was all that I could do."

As the dinner party progressed, there were games. The events rushed over Darcy quickly, and at some point, the party was over.

The guests left, Bingley retreated to the billiard room, still not tired.

As he played a match by himself, the door opened slowly, alarming Bingley.

However, when he saw that it was his sister, Mrs. Hurst, his shoulders slackened.

"I thought you would be asleep with Mr. Hurst, Louisa," Bingley said, "you weren't tired."

"I am, but not like my husband, who can sleep through a hurricane. I came to see you."

Bingley shot a ball, but it didn't go into the pocket.

"What about, especially?"

"Come now, Charles. You have never been secretive about what you are feeling. And if you cannot rely upon your sisters, then who can you rely upon?"

Bingley put down his cue stick.

"Anyone who's advice has not always been sound."

"I am not blind or dense," Mrs. Hurst said, "when you faltered, you were thinking about Jane Bennet, weren't you?"

Bingley did not respond. But his sister knew that his silence was confirmation of this fact.

"You can't keep doing this, Charles. It is your right to be happy. It's been years, and you have the right to fall in love again."

"You don't think that I have tried?" Bingley questioned. "So many worthy women I have met, and I cannot forget her." Bingley's eyes were filled with consternation and self-contempt. "Louisa, I think of her still. She was just so right for me. And I know that you believed yourself correct that she did not care for me, but I cannot believe it."

Mrs. Hurst sat down in a chair by the fireplace, discomforted.

"And here is where it is hard," Mrs. Hurst said, "brother, please do not be angry with me about this. Caroline and I have talked a length on the subject, and we wondered if our observations were misguided. It's easy to say, 'I am right', only for you to wonder that maybe you take a wrong step somewhere. You are aware that perhaps Caroline and I wanted you to marry Miss Darcy. And since we knew that was the better choice than Jane Bennet, maybe we saw what we wanted to see, rather than what was there. I should have let you govern your life. All that I can say is that we meant well. Do you hate me, brother?"

Bingley shook his head.

"No, I do not. Because, as you said, it was ultimately my mistake. I could not have given Miss Bennet up if I had been stronger. But I was weak and allowed you and Darcy to persuade me against my heart. And now here I am. I do not hate you, Louisa. Yet, I do wish that you and Caroline had been better sisters to me back then."

"I know."

"But thank you for apologizing. That means a great deal to me. Hopefully I will find love again. I will try, but you must understand that I cannot force myself. All that I can do is hope."

"That is all that I ask for."

She walked up to her brother and patted his cheek.

"Keep smiling. Because I look forward to the day when that smile will be true." She stepped back. "Merry Christmas brother. My wish is that you find your happiness."

Mrs. Hurst left her brother alone.

At first, he stood there, heavily, until he resumed playing a game by himself.

"What are you feeling now?" Christmas Present asked Darcy. "Anything like that hard word: regret."

"I thought I was helping him."

"And what road is the result of those who had paved it with good intentions? Not the road of perfection, but to perdition."

Christmas Present raised out the music sheet again.

"Come," she said, "we have an ocean to cross."

They dissolved into the musical pattern of life.

As they soared through the air at a rapid pace, the wind whipped about Darcy's face, but it did not break him.

He was more amazed at seeing the ocean down below that he was flying overhead, amazed at the vastness of it.

Music, of course, never left him, as the Spirit laughed —for reasons that Darcy was ignorant of.

The melody was that of the carol, 'Silent Night', as they came upon a large ship that was on the high seas.

It was a merchant vessel, and on deck were musicians playing the song and the passengers were singing, despite the cold and damp on the boat.

Their voices were not alone but were shared by other

voices that rose from ships that were a distance away from each other.

Across the ocean, people were celebrating the winter holidays that they were accustomed to.

It was a great surprise to Darcy. He listened to the moaning of the wind and thought what a harsh thing it was to sail over the watery depths, experience the lonely darkness, where the drink could grow disturbed and swallow them all up.

But instead, merry spirit reached them, even taken away from lands that they were familiar with.

Eventually, Darcy and Christmas Present arrived in a strange land.

Like it had been with London, the city that he looked upon became a mixture of lines, notes, crescendo, and were displayed like sheet music to his eyes.

"Spirit," Darcy said, "where are we?"

"New York, of the United States," Christmas Past explained, as she swiveled the sheet music in her hand. Suddenly, they both lunged to the ground, frightening Darcy as he saw the ground growing closer by the second.

Once they reached it, Darcy covered his face with his hands, to avoid smashing into the earth.

"Darcy?" Christmas Present uttered, "Open your eyes, man."

Darcy opened his eyes to see that he had stopped two inches from the ground and was frozen midair.

After a couple seconds of seeing the ground right underneath him, gravity returned and he fell into the snow, suffering merely a couple of light bruises.

Christmas Present laughed as Darcy struggled, rising to his feet.

"I suppose you rather enjoyed that," Darcy hissed.

"Yes, I rather did," Christmas Present said, beginning to eat a plum.

"Where did you get the plum from?"

Christmas Present gave him a shrewd side-glance.

"Ghost. Remember?"

"Ah," Darcy said, "true. If you can fly me across an ocean in a matter of minutes, then what difficulty is there in a plum?"

After he dusted himself off, he realized that he was standing in front of a lovely townhouse.

"What house is this and what do they have to do with me?" Darcy asked.

"You cannot guess?"

Being deductive, Darcy answered his own question.

"Georgiana lives here."

"Yes, this is her home, with her family. Shall we go in?"

Darcy stood there.

"I've never been in her home before."

"Well, now is your chance to correct that mistake."

They entered through the door, to the sound of many voices. One of these sounded the most familiar as Darcy moved through the many guests who had come for a dinner party.

Through the crowd, he saw her face: it was his sister, Georgiana.

~

"Georgiana!" Darcy cried.

Before him was his sister, Georgiana Mayweather, as she was playing hostess to a Christmas dinner, where many women were elegantly dressed, and men all looked crisp and smart.

"Later this evening," Georgiana began, "after dinner, we have a set of games lined up, and one of my favorite ones was what we often celebrated when back in England."

"My wife brought many things with her from the English countryside," her husband, Mr. Mayweather said, "the games were such another one."

Everyone laughed. Turning to his brother-in-law, Darcy looked at Mr. Mayweather.

"He married Georgiana and took her all the way across the ocean, to New York, where I could never know if she would always be safe. She didn't care that I was worried about her."

"She did care," Christmas Present said, "as you will see. She simply fell in love."

"Yes," Darcy said, bitter, "she fell in love."

Mr. Mayweather looked at the steps behind him and then walked up to Georgiana.

"My love," he said, taking her hand, "I have something alarming to tell you."

"What?" Georgiana asked. "Did the cook burn the ham and turkey? Again."

Everyone laughed once more.

"My dear, we have two mice in the house, who are awake when they should be in bed."

Georgiana perceived, looked at the top of the steps and two children's faces were peeking through the staircase rail-

ings. When they were found out, the children were mortified, and everyone chuckled.

"Two mice indeed," Georgiana declared, going to the
bottom of the steps. "And I think they are watching us.
Fitzwilliam and Cassandra, you have been found out."

"Sorry Mama," little Cassandra apologized.

"Sorry, Mama," Little Fitzwilliam added.

"Fitzwilliam?" Darcy uttered.

"Yes," Christmas Present said, "those are Georgiana's
children, Fitzwilliam and Cassandra."

"My niece and nephew," Darcy remarked, amazed. "I
know that she named her son after me—and that's him."

Darcy focused on the two children, especially his
namesake.

"She named him that," the spirit explained, "out of
love for her brother."

Darcy was silenced and humbled as he looked at the
boy. At last, he turned to Cassandra, and his heart softened
more.

"Cassandra looks like her mother." Darcy turned to the
spirit. "When she was a little girl, Georgiana looked just like
that. I remember it well because Georgiana looked like our
mother. Same face."

"Same good heart."

"We were just having a jolly time watching everything,"
Cassandra said. "It was fun."

"I know, my dears," Georgiana said, "but you have a
long day ahead of you, and your governess will not be
happy when she will be woken up. Never mind, I'll come
and sit with you for a time."

"Don't worry," Mr. Mayweather said, going to the steps and kissing Georgiana's cheek. "I'll take the charge."

He began walking up the first step, to his children.

"You're the better host than I, so I'll make certain that they are tucked in properly." He whispered in her ear. "If the mayor comes before I come back down, make my excuses."

"Very well."

Georgiana's husband went upstairs, taking their children with them. Darcy watched their departing figures, then turned back to Georgiana as she continued to dazzle the guests.

"My husband loves being around our children," Georgiana said, "it was as if he was born wanting to be a father."

"Better than me, I daresay," a guest named Mr. Lonestar said, "children frighten me."

"Even when you were one?" Georgiana asked.

"Especially when I was one," Mr. Lonestar said.

Everyone laughed.

"I have a confession to make," Georgiana informed the crowd, "despite that, in England, once a woman is presented at court, she is given three seasons to find a husband, that whole whirlwind left me...winded. I knew that when I married, I had to bear children, and that idea daunted me."

"It's a common belief that all women must want to get married and have children immediately," another woman said, "But that is not so. We all have the right to question predetermined paths, you know."

"Who is that?" Darcy asked the ghost.

"Her name is Miss Clara Mayweather. She's Georgiana's sister-in-law, and the children's aunt. And Mr. Lonestar is an attorney, who is supposed to be a dedicated bachelor, but he secretly likes Clara. Actually, it's no secret."

"Really?" Mr. Lonestar said, leaning closer to Miss Mayweather. "We are told that cannot be true about women."

"A generalization which ought to be put to rest," Georgiana refuted. "Men have different paths to what they want in life. Like men, women's path ought not to be so singular."

"Precisely, Mr. Lonestar," Miss Mayweather said, "you like to rule your life. Is it really so hard thinking a lady considered such as well?"

Mr. Lonestar grinned at her.

"Whenever Miss Mayweather speaks, I cannot refuse for too long."

Everyone cooed.

"Really, Mr. Lonestar," Miss Mayweather said, blushing, "what can I say to that?"

"Thank you," he responded, "and really, you must call me Harry. All my good friends call me Harry."

"Am I a good friend?"

"Yes. Very."

"Well, then... Mr. Harry, thank you."

Everyone was enjoying another round of punch.

"Your sister is a delightful hostess," Present pointed out.

"Yes, she is." Darcy was astounded. "She has played hostess before, but never to this degree. After all, she was still very shy."

"She was still full young, in her teenage years."

"True. She has aged and it must have brought her confidence."

"As well as being a woman who came to the other side of the world, took a risk that was successful, and therefore had to develop on her own. It gave her the chance to create herself, rather than merely doing what was expected."

"That's what would have happened if she had remained."

"How do you know?"

They were interrupted when there was a knock on the door.

The butler informed them all that the mayor had arrived.

All the guests were excited, and Mr. Mayweather came down the stairs just in time.

They were all assembled, and the mayor entered, with his wife and siblings.

Georgiana and her husband greeted them warmly, and the mayor was disposed to enjoy himself.

His wife greeted Georgiana comfortably, and it was evident that they were good friends.

"Georgiana," she began, "I have looked forward to this dinner for some time."

"I was worried that you all would not come."

"Fortunately," the mayor explained, "my business was concluded sooner than I had expected, that gave us time to return from New Hampshire. Which is good, because if I made us miss this event, my wife would have had my head."

"It's true," she responded, lightly, "I would have. So, tell me, dear Georgiana. Have your family managed to come from England because we love your stories about them. And we will always be curious to meet them."

"Not this Christmas, sadly," Georgiana informed her and the room, "but in three months' time, your curiosity will be satisfied. Around Easter, my cousin, Colonel Fitzwilliam will be coming down with his new wife, and she will bring two of her sisters with us. Believe me, the Colonel and those ladies will be a charming set that you will never forget. And I know that they will love you all."

Everyone replied in the affirmative.

"Now," Georgiana said, "we have a meal that I think will satisfy your heart's content, and when we are done, there is a game that you must play. Has anyone heard of the game, 'The Minister's Cat'."

Everyone shook their heads.

"It is a game that we played at Rosings Park whenever things got a little dull, and I cannot wait to see how you enjoy it—or don't enjoy it."

The butler nodded to her, she squeezed her husband's hand and announced that it was time for dinner.

As they all filed into the dining room, Georgiana linked arms with her husband.

"The one delight of New York society is that I don't have to worry about arranging who goes into the dining room first, and who sits where," Georgiana whispered. "I don't have to worry over this earl or lady being placed, and what station of peerage comes first."

"Yes," Mr. Mayweather said, tapping her arm lovingly, "we here are too simple to make those things complicated."

Georgiana chuckled, but her husband sensed something

more. He knew that she was secretly wistful about something.

"I'm sorry that your brother still hasn't come."

"Thank you, my dear. I don't know why I get my hopes up every year. If he would only come and see how we are, he would see that I made the correct choice. I want my children to know him."

"You cannot help but hope, and that makes sense."

"Thank you. And for something else."

"For what?"

"For being the man that I married, and not a whole different person after we exchanged vows. For being what you promised me."

"Always."

They walked into the dinner, where a wonderful meal was prepared.

Darcy watched as everyone was enjoying themselves and how happy his sister looked.

And her happiness produced a grander beauty to her features than ever before. Also, being a mother, she had gained weight, and it filled out her figure a little more, making her appear womanlier.

"She is happy," Christmas Present announced.

"Yes," Darcy admitted, "she is."

"And you are not."

Darcy looked at the spirit but could find no answer.

"It is time to move on," Christmas Present said, touching Darcy's shoulder.

"Please, spirit," Darcy implored. "My sister is separated from me, by an ocean. Can you give me more time?"

Present did not speak, but only nodded, her eyes turning softer.

After dinner, they all lined up and began to play the game 'The Minister's Cat'.

One person would say 'the Minister's cat is a___ cat'.

The game was simple, but also rather difficult, because it required a creative mind.

Once you gave a description of the cat, the person to your left had to give another description, using the same first letter, and it would continue down the circle.

If you could not think of a word, you were out.

"The Minister's cat is a lovely cat," Georgiana began.

"The Minister's cat is a lazy cat," her husband said.

"The Minister's cat is a lonely cat," Miss Mayweather said.

"The Minister's cat is a lucky cat," the mayor's wife said.

"The Minister's cat is a laughing cat," the mayor said.

"The Minister's cat is a lusty cat," Mr. Lonestar said.

"The Minister's cat is a…" another guest began but he could not think of the right word. After counting to five, he still could not think of anything and groaned when he was out.

Since this was a game of quick wit, Darcy began to take part in it as well and would make guesses. When others could not think of an answer, and he did, he took pleasure in it.

When the game was over, Darcy laughed.

"I would have won!" he cried. They were unable to hear him, but in fact, he had more guesses than the entire company.

When it occurred to him that he had enjoyed himself, Darcy sat down in a chair that no one occupied.

"I was…happy."

Christmas Present approached him and sat down to his left.

"Yes," Christmas Present said, "I suppose you were."

She raised up sheet music.

"It is time for us to see one more Christmas day."

Before he obeyed and touched the paper, he looked at Georgiana.

"Thank you," he said, "thank you, sister."

Darcy touched the music and once more they disappeared, being hurled back across the ocean.

Back home.

When they appeared again, this time it was back in London, in Colonel Fitzwilliam's townhouse.

Everyone was running back and forth to a hiding place.

"This way, Richard!" Kitty Bennet said, "let us hide behind the sofa. "And where is Lizzy?"

"Here I come."

Darcy turned sharply to see Elizabeth come rushing down the stairs, with Jane behind her.

Dressed in lovely gowns, Elizabeth looked even more beautiful than ever before.

"Elizabeth," Darcy declared as she rushed through him.

"I don't see how successful we shall be," Elizabeth said, "Lydia will know that we are home. But I am not in the mood to be a kill-a-joy, so let us get to it."

In the house was Colonel Fitzwilliam, his elder brother, Frederick Fitzwilliam, his parents the Earl and Lady Fitzwilliam of Matlock. There were, overall, twenty other guests, including four of the five Bennet sisters, Jane, Elizabeth, Mary and Kitty.

Soon, there was a knock on the door.

Everyone hid behind sofas, curtains, closets, and other rooms.

Even the Earl and Lady Fitzwilliam, influenced by their sons, partook in the mischief.

The butler opened the door, and from their hiding place, they heard the boisterous tones of the youngest Bennet sister, Lydia.

"Merry Christmas, Danvers," Lydia said to the butler as they were escorted in.

"Thank you, Mrs. Denny," Danvers responded, "and Merry Christmas to you both."

"Thank you," Captain Denny, Lydia's husband, added.

"Danvers," Lydia said, "I have heard the most astonishing thing about you."

"And what would that be, pray tell?"

Lydia laughed.

"That your last name is not really Danvers. That it is Biggerstaff."

Danvers chuckled.

"Come now, tell us the truth," Captain Denny said, "is it not so?"

"Oh, very well," Danvers said. "Yes, it is. It simply had to be changed because the name Biggerstaff is too—unique for when you are into service."

"How strange. To be a butler, you had to give up your

last, name," Lydia said. "Fiddle-dee. I liked both of my last names and would never give them up."

"Now," Denny said, "take us to the party that we are obviously late for."

"Of course," Danvers said.

"It's really my fault that we are late," Lydia said, following him in, "I don't know how Denny puts up with me."

"I am certain that your family can forgive you by this point," Denny encouraged, then he noted the silence. "Well, it's rather quiet in here for a party. We shall have to be reserved; I see."

Danvers led them into the parlor, where, to their knowledge, there was no one there.

"Are we in the wrong room?" Denny asked.

Suddenly, everyone jumped out from their hiding places, or the other rooms.

It made Lydia and Denny jump. They both laughed.

"Well, that was a good joke!" Lydia said as Kitty rushed up to her and they both twirled each other around.

"You have no notion how long it took me to convince them to pull that prank," Kitty said. "But I knew that you would like it."

"I did. It made me jump!"

"And how about you, Denny?" Kitty asked, "tell me, you did like it, brother."

"I did," Denny said, taking Kitty's hand. "Being teased makes me feel more like part of the family."

"That's the way to do it."

"Sister, you look remarkably well this evening," Lydia said.

"As do you."

"Married life suits me, but nothing beats being a fiancée!"

"As irrational as that sounds, I feel like I have more color to my cheeks."

Darcy moved away from the spirit and approached Elizabeth and Jane, who had stood back for a time.

It was natural, considering that Kitty and Lydia had always been close.

Further down the way, Mary was standing next to her husband, Mr. Collins, who had already taken over Longbourn for quite some time.

"I confess," Mr. Collins said, moving forward, "that being a wife is the fullest a lady's life can find the ultimate satisfaction, much more than that of a fiancée."

"My sisters are just speaking in jest, dearest," Mary said, and taking Jane into consideration. Despite being the loveliest of the five, she was the only one to have never been married.

Lydia laughed, but Kitty was a little more sensitive.

"Come now, brother," Kitty said to Mr. Collins, "surely we ladies can have many titles that bring satisfaction. Plurality of labels, and identity, is a good thing, as you know very well, yourself."

"Excellently put, dearest," Colonel Fitzwilliam said to Kitty.

"Oh, well then," Mr. Collins said, "quite so, Colonel. Quite so."

Tearing his eyes away from Elizabeth, Darcy focused on Jane. While the eldest Bennet sister was serene as ever, there was something hidden, almost like a shadow that lurked under the surface, and Jane had lost her bloom that augmented her beauty.

She bore the jokes with fortitude and amusement, but he could tell that she was hurt.

Elizabeth went behind Jane, wrapped her arms around her, and held her in an embrace.

Darcy drew close to them both, so that he could hear.

"You know Lydia does not mean it," Lizzy began, "She's just not thinking before she speaks."

"I am not unhappy or upset with her," Jane said, "she just has high spirits. And even I know that there is something wonderful about having the love of your life and keeping it."

"Yes, you do. We both do. But you deserved the most."

"Do not worry about me, Lizzy. I chose where I am now, and I will always be happy for my sisters, as I was happy for you. But for my part, it is harder to be a widow than to be single. I wished that you had been given better fortune, my poor Lizzy."

"As I feel with you."

"Do you ever wonder," Jane asked, "what life would have been like if things had turned out differently. If the men in our past had made different choices."

"Andy by that," Elizabeth said, "you mean by if they were not fools and had made the right choices."

"You put it better."

"I'm not afraid to use crueler and more cutting words," Elizabeth said, laughing. They moved a little further away from the party, so that they could have a more intimate discussion.

"Well, if one were to give into the great Goddess that is

Honesty," Elizabeth continued, "then yes, I do think of the past often, when we were at Longbourn, all five of us, young and hearty—and dreaming of a love that seemed like it would come true. And, for us, for a few minutes, it did. But life took us in a stranger route."

"You found love again."

"I loved Jacob," Elizabeth said, "I did and cherished what we had. However, I will not deny that Darcy was my first large love. You and I had our infatuations before he and Bingley came into Hertfordshire, but they were something more. Despite that I cursed them both when they left us, and that maybe I might have dreamed some very horrible fates to them—" Jane could not help but smile at that remark—"they were our truly big loves."

"They were," Jane said, "they gave us good memories, before the future that never was."

"They did. So, I decided to view them as our big adventure before we were given a terrible life lesson and learned more about the ways of the world."

"That's why I could not ever forget Mr. Bingley. The adventure was too beautiful for there to be anything else. I know that I should have moved on, but I just—"

"No one judged you."

"Even when I must be labeled an old maid."

"Did you not listen to what Kitty said? We women reserve the right to have more than one label, and that those labels are not wrong. Being single is a virtue, in its own right."

"Jane and Lizzy!" Lydia said, approaching them. "Honestly! When are you going to embrace your little sister?"

She rushed to them, and they all held each other.

"Mary!" Lydia said.

"I come, I come," Mary said, also joining the embrace.

"Now that is a lovely image, do you not agree?" Mr. Denny asked Colonel Fitzwilliam. "The Bennet sisters are reunited."

"Indeed, we are," Jane said, as they separated, and Kitty completed the scene by standing next to them.

"I too enjoy seeing the five of you standing together," Colonel Fitzwilliam said, then he turned to his parents and brother, "They complete the scene when they are united."

"Indeed," Lord Fitzwilliam said, "I think that you all would grace the halls of St. James's Court."

When hearing that, all the Bennet sisters laughed, because they recalled someone.

"I think there is a certain knight, back in Hertfordshire who agrees with you," Elizabeth added.

"She's talking about Sir William Lucas, of Lucas Lodge," Darcy informed the ghost. "He was forever going on and on about when he was presented at court and elevated."

"In a world where ranks and peerage are everything," Christmas Present said. "Was he more vexing than the rest?"

Darcy did not respond but only watched the scene.

Lydia apologized to Elizabeth for Jacob's death and Elizabeth being a widow. Though he died six months ago, it still felt quite recent.

As soon as Elizabeth expressed her thanks, and expressed her missing Jacob, Lydia turned to Kitty and the Colonel.

"This is a Christmas Party. Please tell me that there shall be dancing. I long for a dance."

"Then dance you shall," Frederick Fitzwilliam said. "We shall have dancing tonight, won't we, Richard?"

"That was one of the first things that we planned for," Colonel Fitzwilliam said, looking at Kitty. "You were right."

"Oh yes," Kitty said, "put a lot of women in a room with men who are of the same number, and you've got the perfect mixture for the activity. And for this, you are my fiancé, so I will be bold and do something extreme."

"What would that be?"

"Ask you to dance with me," Kitty said, pretending to be the gentleman in this case. "Colonel Fitzwilliam, might I have the pleasure of taking your hand, for the first two dances?"

Everyone gave teasing tones, and Colonel Fitzwilliam blushed.

"This is one of those moments, where I knew that I was happy to propose marriage to her when I did," he informed everyone, "because if I didn't do it sooner, I believe that she would have proposed first."

"How clever of you to know that," Kitty said. "I was even considering getting down on one knee."

The group laughed.

"But first," Lady Fitzwilliam said, taking Kitty's hand, "food, then dancing."

"Mama," Colonel Fitzwilliam said, kissing her cheek, "thank you for playing hostess instead of myself, because I really was not motivated."

Lady Fitzwilliam made them all file into dinner.

Between being kind and partly because he had a softness for Jane Bennet, Frederick Fitzwilliam offered her his arm to go into dinner.

Mr. Collins took Mary and Elizabeth's arms on both sides and escorted them in. When watching Mr. Collins being gallant, Darcy felt a tinge of jealousy swell up inside of him.

"Delightful," Lydia said, "for I am famished. Kitty and Colonel, please celebrate Christmas every year. Denny and I will always love to come."

"Lydia will never say it, so I will say it for her," Denny said, "she misses being around you all more."

"Your husband has to reveal the better part of your nature," Elizabeth said. "Lydia, you will never change."

"Well, I did stop growing when I turned seventeen. Good, because I am happy that I didn't get taller. And where is Miss de Bourgh? I was told that she was coming."

"Sadly," Lady Fitzwilliam said, "her health is indifferent, and she could not join us."

"How unfortunate. I would hate to be sick all the time. Oh well! Perhaps I can wait till next year to finally meet her."

Even though he was invisible, Darcy was so happy that he did not have to see his cousin.

He was still too embarrassed.

As they ate, Darcy marveled at his aunt and uncle Fitzwilliam, the Earl and Lady of Matlock.

"I cannot fathom it," he observed. "Matlock is one of the greatest estates in England. Richard came from a great family, but being a second son, he was always told to marry well, because he could not choose just anyone. He needed an heiress. Then he is given a grand inheritance from a distant relative, chooses Miss Kitty, and his parents accept it. I thought that they would have been angry."

"Colonel Fitzwilliam did something unexpected. Since his wealth came from another direction, his parents had no control over it, and he had the freedom to marry who he wanted. Besides, remember what your cousin would also say. Being the second son, he often despised having to consider money when he married, and that he could not marry where he chose. If he had wealth, the woman's dowry didn't matter to him. Nor did her position in society because he didn't fear society. After all, he had family."

Darcy looked at Elizabeth, who symbolized his shame.

"Like I did," Darcy said.

"Yes. The family that you never come to see—many people do not have such good fortune, and you do not value it properly. Look around you. You could be here."

"I think... I do wish to be."

"Good," Christmas Present said, "because, if you did not, then it shall be set down that, in the sight of heaven, you are more worthless and less fit to live than millions who have been given much less, attempt to make more, and lose anyway, due to the great wheel of life that turns them so. Count your blessings, man."

When Christmas Present spoke that way, her eyes were fierce and insistent, where she bore her intention into Darcy's spirit.

He was becoming humbled, and more and more, he was accepting the many errors of his ways.

During the dinner, conversation was copious, and Lord and Lady Fitzwilliam were talking passionately among themselves.

Colonel Fitzwilliam and Kitty were too much engaged in each other's company to notice, but Frederick Fitzwilliam, the eldest brother, noticed.

"What do you talk so animatedly about, I wonder?" Frederick asked his parents. "I cannot help it but be curious about it, Mama, because it interests you a great deal. Nay, I insist on knowing your meaning, sir and madam."

"We were just thinking of our nephew," Lady Fitzwilliam said, "your cousin."

"Ah, the mountain that refuses to crack." Frederick Fitzwilliam turned to Jane. "Miss Bennet, did you happen to become well-acquainted with my cousin when he stayed in Hertfordshire?"

Jane exchanged a glance with Elizabeth, who looked down at her plate, being prepared to hear about the man who had walked out of her life. Time helped it get easier, but there will always be a slight pain in those sorts of circumstances.

"Yes and no," Jane said. "I made his acquaintance, but we very rarely talked."

"Well, being his cousin, I can attest that Darcy was once a very different man, before he became the misanthrope that he is now. I have my moments of ill-judgment, but he's had an ocean of them."

Colonel Fitzwilliam, Kitty and Mary also glanced at Elizabeth, equally worried for her.

"There was a time where he was open, warm, rational, and considerate. Now he's morphed into a gnarled oak, that is twisted and perverse. I've done something that I rarely do, which is write him letters. When I did, each one felt as if he was slipping away from the family."

"Frederick," Lord Fitzwilliam said, "this is hardly the discussion at Christmastime."

"Why not? Everyone at the table hear knows that my cousin, who was once a promising man in the ton, has turned into a cold and pessimistic malcontent."

Everyone at the table even nodded, tapped their glasses, and said, 'here, here."

"I mean, consider it Mother and Father," Frederick continued. "His wealth is even of no use to him, except that he uses his life of luxury to retreat from the rest of the world. And who suffers from his ill whims? Himself, as always. He does not even dine with us for my brother's engagement party. Now that's taking the role of cynic to the extreme."

"Forgive me for speaking, despite not being in the family," said a guest to Colonel Fitzwilliam and Kitty, "but he had better give you both the best present when he comes to your wedding."

Colonel Fitzwilliam and Kitty looked discomforted.

Another guest read their expressions and spoke before she considered.

"Mr. Darcy is coming to your wedding, is he not?" she asked. When she got no answer, the silence was painful.

"Is this where you find the word 'regret' coming to mind," Christmas Present whispered in Darcy's ear. "Especially now considering that you do not have 'duty' to hide behind. It's your duty to come to your cousin's wedding. But you do not do it."

"I cannot," Darcy extoled, his voice cracking a little.

"Why not?"

"Because the answer hurts."

"I shall give it to you, later," she said, and once more, they listened.

The woman who asked the question, realized that the answer was not a good one, so she randomly complimented the food.

It was a well-meaning gesture, but the damage had been done.

"My cousin has grown to despise weddings," Colonel Fitzwilliam said.

"Which I cannot accept," Mary said, plain and simply, "pardon me, but since you are marrying my sister, I have a right to believe that he ought to do right by you both and recognize your happy day."

"And if it hurts him," Lydia said, "then he had better get over it."

"I wish that he would come," Kitty said, eyeing Elizabeth quickly. "But perhaps it is best for him not to impose his company on us, if he will not like the event."

"Precisely," Elizabeth said. "When one takes it upon themselves to be taciturn, we are best left to our company, and he is best left to his bedrooms, where he could do no damage."

"True," Lady Fitzwilliam uttered. "But the good news is that their cousin, Anne de Bourgh, is coming from Rosings Park, especially, to witness the desirable event."

The conversation shifted to Lady Anne de Bourgh, who now bore the title, would be at the wedding, leading to the dinner finding its merriment again.

"And for our honeymoon," Colonel Fitzwilliam announced, "we are going to New York to visit Georgiana in March."

"Oh, you fortunate pair," Lydia said. "I would like to go."

"I would like the idea of us all going, but I worry that I would be overstepping if I asked her."

"Actually," Colonel Fitzwilliam said, with a mischievous look in his eye, "I already asked her."

Kitty's eyes widened.

"You did?"

"I asked if she would find it acceptable if all the Bennet girls would accompany me and visit her. She said yes."

Jane, Elizabeth, Mary, Kitty and Lydia all exclaimed. Denny and Mr. Collins were excluded, not due to inconsideration but because Denny could not be spared from his duties, and Mr. Collins still had to run Longbourn.

This led to merriment and discussion of what life for Georgiana was like and the joys of traveling and being born anew.

After dinner, the dancing began.

Mary was eager to play the music while the dance commenced, with Mr. Collins turning the pages.

Frederick stood up with Jane, Elizabeth with another guest at the party, Kitty with the Colonel, Lydia with Denny, and Lord and Lady Fitzwilliam danced as well.

There were other partners who stood up together, but Darcy's attention remained fixed on Elizabeth.

Mary began playing, the dancers took their places and began to dance the Polka.

When Elizabeth began dancing, her beauty was apparent to him, and he found himself mesmerized again.

Slowly, he moved away from the wall and placed himself directly in the same place as her partner.

She was seeing the man that she danced with, but Darcy was there, the entire time, seeing her from his place.

At first, he assumed that he would hold her hands in place as best as he could, but he realized that he was able to place his hand on her hand, and his other hand on her hip.

He could touch her.

Amazed, he turned to Christmas Present.

"A gift for you," Present said to him, "dance on, and feel the music."

In her arms, Darcy danced with her.

Enjoying her touch, Darcy fell in love with her... all over again.

For as Elizabeth had been known for saying it, dancing was the food of love, even if one's partner was barely tolerable.

The dance continued, and Darcy counted his blessings as he saw her fine eyes light up at the amusement and dreamt of having her as a wife.

If only he could go back in time...

Sadly, there were some things that even Christmas Present could not do.

As he turned Elizabeth, the scene around them seemed to spin, the world fell away and dissolved before he knew it.

When he opened his eyes, he was in the parlor in his townhouse.

"What?!" he roared.

He turned and Christmas Present was placing her sheet music back on the pianoforte.

"Spirit," Darcy said, "please, can you not take me back? I enjoyed it all. I wanted to stay."

"Then that means that I have done much good this Christmas Eve," she responded, "but my time on this earth is very brief, and soon it comes to an end."

"But I have learned much from you. I can learn more."

"In life, there can sometimes be a tomorrow," she said, "and then, you can continue the lesson on your own. Especially when it's time for me to leave you with an answer to the question that I asked you earlier."

Darcy knew, but he was still scared.

As such, he moved to the other side of the room and looked out of the window.

"Look, man!" Present cried, with such a force that it shook the room. "Here! Look here!"

It was so powerful that it forced Darcy to turn around and look upon her.

"I know the answer," Darcy said, "you do not have to tell me. I know it!"

"But you must hear it."

Darcy held the wall, to steady himself for the truth.

"It was your duty to go to your sister's wedding. It is your duty to go to your cousin's. Duty rules your life, but now you turn your back upon it. The answer is there, for you to see. You cannot go because they are walking the path that you should have and didn't. They made the decision that you wanted to make and could not. You cannot go, because you will see the life you ought to have had, but never shall. And it hurts you to see it. You know that it will break you."

Darcy closed his eyes and hit the wall with his fists.

"I know. You have told me, now be done with it."

"No. Listen!"

A beautiful melody began to play, and it filled Darcy up.

"It's beautiful," Darcy said, as it filled his heart. "What is it?"

"That is the sound of good intentions gone right," Present continued. "The sound of walking down the path that was right to walk along. It is the sound of humanity whenever someone finds their path, chooses it, and walks down it fearlessly, finding completion in themselves and those around them. That song is the many souls who died with no more regrets, because they lived their life to the fullest, and the kindest."

Suddenly, the music changed to something dreadful. Hauntingly curious, but still *dreadful*, as it filled Darcy with doubt and fear.

"Why has the music changed? What is it? It is terrifying."

"That tune also belongs to humankind. Painful and frightening, is it not?"

"Yes. It disturbs my mind."

"That music is the sound of intentions gone wrong. Of the many cries of people who made the wrong choices. Who turned right when they ought to have turned left. Who turned left when they ought to have turned right. And gone right when they should have gone center."

Darcy looked out into the night sky and felt the sorrow.

"This tune is the pain of the billions of human souls who wish they could have gone back and do the right thing that their heart told them to. It's the song of regret."

Darcy felt the music wash over him and affect him greatly.

"I leave you now," Christmas Present said, "at the turning of the page. You shall now meet another. Go on, and know her better…"

The ghost dissolved.

CHAPTER 13
The Third of the Spirits

When Darcy was left alone, he felt forlorn and listless.

"Spirit," he uttered, "your leaving was sooner than expected, and I have more questions. Spirit!"

He called around, but there was no response.

He began to pace back and forth, wondering what he ought to do next. As he did so, he noticed the mirror that was against the wall.

While one could easily overlook this, Darcy was particularly attentive to all that occurred.

After all, he had grown accustomed to expecting an apparition, making him more alert.

But the mirror—the room was in it, as was the furniture —but not him.

He moved back and forth in front of it, but his reflection was not there.

He drew close to it, waiting to see him staring back at himself, but it never materialized.

Then slowly... and surely, a shape began to appear.

It was the outline of a woman's face and her neck.

Perplexed, Darcy stood back, moving away from the mirror, but watching what unfolded before him.

The woman's shape grew more defined, but not in its entirety, as her face moved through the mirror, then her neck, arms, torso, legs and levitated onto the floor.

His eyes widened in amazement as he beheld the third spirit.

It was a lady, that much was certain. Her outline gave all the indication of that. However, she was so much more.

Where there ought to be skin, hair, and a large and well-made gown with a large and wide skirt, it was all pages.

Pages with words scribbled upon them.

Her skin was striking, being completely black pages with white words written all over them. Her dress was all made of white pages with black words scribbled everywhere, layers upon layers of paper, making up many volumes of the skirt portion. Her fingers were long and pointy at the tips.

Every now and again, the words on her skin changed into a different one. Letters that would vanish and then reappear differently.

And she, like all the pages that made her up, glowed in the darkness, illuminating all, and she felt as if she floated along, despite still walking on the floor.

At first, Darcy just stood there, with her staring directly at him.

Amazed at her surreal beauty and of seeing something that was all new to him, Darcy sat down gently, humbled.

"Am I in the presence of the Ghost of Christmas Yet to Come?" Darcy asked.

The Spirit did not answer, but only took a step forward, and looked at him.

While there were no visible eyes, he could still see the outline of where they would be. When looking at them, her meaning fell into his brain, a strange and beautiful piece of heartbreaking music filled his body and so did her words.

Darcy clutched his head, feeling his presence in her mind, as his heart was stirred by the music, she filled him with.

Not only that, but his emotions felt like they were alive, and somewhat on fire.

At first, he was confused about how this could be, but then he began to understand, because the ghost was explaining it to him. In his thoughts.

When he opened his eyes again, he was still seated, looking up at the incredible ghost.

"You cannot speak, can you?" he asked.

She didn't respond, and that was confirmation enough.

"No, you cannot, but I feel your presence in my mind. I hear every response to my questions from a voice that's not made of sound, but emotion."

She leaned her head forward, and suddenly Darcy's emotions erupted within him. She made his brain re-experience every happy, sad, passionate, and vicious moment of his life.

The music in his soul weighed heavier as well, forcing

his knees to buckle until he fell on the floor, clutching his head, trying to keep it from splitting.

"My whole life!" he cried, "you're making me feel every emotion that I have felt, and it's ripping me apart. I can't feel all this at once. Please, spirit! Please!"

Through his closed eyes, he felt the light glow more. Despite the pain, he managed to open them as he saw the ghost glide forward. Her movements were graceful and elegant as she leaned down over him, and placed her hands on both sides of his face.

Her fingers were warm and inviting, as the outline of her 'eyes' closed and she focused.

Darcy felt her presence in his mind more, but not as another force that was overwhelming his brain. No, she was sharing the pain he was feeling and causing a link between them that would remain.

She was lessening the load, and sharing his grief, and disappointments. The music that was pounding in his ears was no longer harsh, but lighter and gentle.

When Darcy was able to open his eyes, he looked into her face and lost himself in it.

"My lady," he said.

She removed her hands from his face, but impulsively, he took one of her hands in his.

"Empathy," he determined, "you are empathy."

Christmas Yet to Come gently moved her fingers over his palm, as if it was performing a dance around it.

With every feeling, Darcy had a quick flash of every time that Elizabeth and he touched during dances. The joy and exhilaration of it returned to him, followed by the pain of when he would never feel it again.

When Darcy looked into the spirit's face, he knew that their expressions were the same.

They both were feeling that anguish.

"I never thought that an Empath was ever anything else but fiction. But spirit, here you are."

Gently, she removed her hand from his and gracefully moved to the other side of the room, breathing in deeply, feeling his inner dread.

"When I am afraid, so are you," Darcy continued, "and when I am heartbroken, so are you. My feelings are your feelings."

Darcy struggled to stand up, but he clutched the chair next to him, for support.

"You are here to show me the future. Is that so?"

Almost like moving through water, she looked back at him, and her answer was in his thoughts.

"Yes, you are," he responded. He closed his eyes, over-come. "You are here to draw my feelings, my loves, my hates, my emotions, all of it—out of me. And we shall feel it together. And because of such spirit, I fear you more than any other specter that I have seen. Where they showed me things to stir my heart, you are here to wring it out and lay it down for me to hurt."

She did not speak, but he heard her answer, all the same.

"I know," he added, "that you will be there to feel all that I experience along with me. At least I am not alone."

She touched her own face, gesturing to where her eyes would have been.

"Yes," he said, "I see it properly; I do not want to be alone. Therefore, conduct me where you will. Especially since I know that your purpose is to do me good. Lead on, spirit, lead on."

Once more, she glided up to him, raised up her arm and placed her hand on his chest, where his heart was.

A wind swept around them, as her dress rustled and grew. Where the room once was, it was like pages from her dress were growing of large proportions as they covered everything.

Darcy and the ghost were surrounded by white pages with many words written on them.

Despite the incredible change of scenery, he still focused on the ghost who was looking back up at him.

With her hand still covering his heart, he could attend to nothing else but her.

After all, his heart was now also hers as the words on her face shifted around and only one word was written on her cheek:

REGRET

The room appeared again, and this time, it was Christmas Day in Georgiana's home, in New York.

On the desk was a newspaper. Darcy saw that it was the year 1860. The house was decorated with all the holiday ornaments, it was beautiful, and outside there was snow on the ground.

Georgiana was not alone, of course. Her husband was there, and she was surrounded by three children, who were playing with the other children in the house.

Among them were Colonel Fitzwilliam and Kitty's children.

And the Colonel and Kitty were not the only ones who had come to see Georgiana. Also, in attendance was Mary with Mr. Collins, who was offering to read up a prayer from the holy book for when dinner would occur.

Two of their children were also present as well.

And then, right on cue, there was a knock on the door. Soon, Elizabeth, Jane and two gentlemen entered, carrying some pudding and fruit.

"Don't worry," Jane said, looking lovely, "we found a grocery shop still open and got more pudding and fruit for the day."

All the children roared out in happiness.

"How has my little Nathaniel been doing?" Elizabeth asked, approaching a little boy.

"We were playing Sardines," Nathaniel said, "and Mama and Papa, I was not very good."

"I'm certain that you were good," Jane offered, "and how about my little dears."

"Son," one of the gentlemen said, standing next to Elizabeth, "you are too hard on yourself at times."

"Who does he get it from?" Elizabeth questioned, pinching the man's arm.

"Me," the other man laughed, which immediately caught Darcy's attention.

"Who is he to her?" Darcy asked the ghost. She didn't speak the answer, but he heard it from her, all the same. "Elizabeth married again." He looked at Elizabeth's second husband, and then he also looked at the man with Jane, who both bent down to kiss two children who were also in the party. "And Jane married eventually."

As he looked at Jane, Darcy felt an inner sense of shame. If Bingley knew this, he would be even more despondent. What was even more was that Jane appeared to be happy with her choice of husband.

"They both married," Darcy uttered, "and found their way—" He was cut off when he felt the spirit's presence in his mind and heart. His emotions were more awake than ever, and she felt his anguish.

"Yes," Darcy answered what she conveyed, "I do feel quite broken now, and—"

He trailed off when he looked at the little boy, Nathaniel, who Elizabeth and her husband were overseeing and fixing his collar.

"That's her son, isn't it?" Darcy choked. He felt the ghost's answer. "Yes. Of course it is."

While still watching little Nathaniel, Darcy backed against the wall. At first, the pain was slow, but as Christmas Yet to Come drew closer to him, she gave him no choice but to delve deeper into his emotions, and the agony grew more and more excruciating.

"If life had been different," Darcy professed, "he could have been mine. That could have been my son."

The ghost linked to him, as his own guilt, shame, and humiliation had transferred to her.

She empathized, helping him feel not alone.

Darcy turned to her; his face distorted as they experienced all these sensations together.

"Spirit, this could have been my future. This could have been my life."

The ghost raised up her hand and Darcy, eager to have her hold him, placed his hand on hers. Closing her fingers around him, the shadow offered him solace.

He felt the easing of his grief escape himself and drift

into her as she transformed it into hope. A fleeting hope that all was not lost.

"Thank you."

He looked back at Nathaniel and Elizabeth.

"The wife and the son," he uttered, "what fools' mortals like me shall be…"

Christmas Yet to Come placed her hand on his shoulder, the pages from her gown stretched, covered the scene as they shifted to another time in the future.

When they appeared again, it was in front of another house that Darcy was familiar with.

"I recall this place," Darcy said, "it's the home of the Hudsons."

Darcy turned to the ghost, his expression light. "It was a delight seeing them before and—"

When he looked at the ghost, the link now was ever present and lingering. What she sensed, he sensed. And he sensed sadness.

"Something has happened, hasn't it?"

The music that flowed and ebbed, lending description to what they were experiencing, and Darcy felt the somber tones that crept out of the spirit.

"How terrible is it?" he asked her.

The letters on her face rearranged to show one word:

LOSS

She gestured behind him, and Darcy turned in time to see Mr. Hudson walk down the road, toward the house.

His walk was heavy, and there seemed to be a shadow on his face, displaying what occurred underneath.

Everyone walks around, wearing a mask, to disguise their innermost thoughts. With Hudson being one of the best butlers that England had to offer, he rarely ever showed anything on his face except persistence in doing his duty well and maintaining the proper flow of the household.

Now, he was anything else but content.

In fact, if Darcy had not known any better, he could have sworn that Hudson had been crying, at some point.

When he reached the front door to his house, at first, he had every intention of placing the key in the door, but he froze.

It was a weighty position, and Darcy could tell that Hudson was experiencing dread.

"He doesn't want to see something," Darcy said, "and I don't think that I want to see it, either."

The ghost walked forward, looked back at him, and her actions pulled him on, following Hudson into the house.

When they entered, Hudson had just announced that he was home, but it was in a meek and quiet sort of manner.

After all, there was no need, because most of the family were sitting down in the parlor, equally cast low in behavior.

Elinor and Martha rushed to him, taking his coat, hat, and gloves.

When looking at their desperate movements, Hudson was even more apprehensive.

"Elinor and Martha. She's not—"

"Mama still lives," Elinor said, "but only just."

"I was worried that I was not going to make it in time!" Hudson said, racing past his sister, dashing up the steps and bursting into his mother's room.

When he did, he saw Marianne, sitting there, holding her mother's hand.

"John," Marianne said.

"I came as soon as I could." Hudson rushed to his mother's side, knelt, and took her hand in his. "Mother!"

Mrs. Hudson's eyes were closed, and her breathing was raspy. Her face was pale white, and sweat was dripping at the base of her hairline.

She was nearing the end.

"Mama," Hudson stressed, tears almost filling his eyes, "it's me. It's John. I'm sorry that I could not come when I was called. I could not get my employer to give me a full day."

"I didn't?" Darcy asked the ghost, mortified. "His mother was ill, and I did not allow it?"

Christmas Yet to Come sat down in a nearby chair, in despair. Darcy's shame was hers.

"What did I become?" he asked the ghost, though in a way, he was asking himself.

When hearing her son's voice, Mrs. Hudson managed to pull herself away from the inevitable for just a little bit longer.

With every ounce of the life she had left, she opened her eyes, breathing heavily and clinging to life, through all the hopelessness.

"John…"

Hearing his mother's voice one last time brought animation to Mr. Hudson's face.

"Mama," he whispered, full of all the affection of a son's love.

Her eyes lit up, briefly—too briefly when bidding farewell to your children, as all lights go out, since they must. Yet, her fight was powerfully rendered before her eyes closed again.

And didn't open after.

Mrs. Hudson was gone, and her son and daughter were there to see it fade.

Marianne cried out, in grief.

This sent Elinor upstairs, bursting in to see that their mother was now in heaven.

"Mother!" Hudson cried, pressing his face against hers, for one last touch of the woman who gave him her life, love, and lifeforce.

Christmas Yet to Come's influence had been so effective that Darcy felt Hudson's anguish as he lay by his mother, who looked at peace.

As the ghost moved forward, Darcy echoed her actions. Floating through the scene, she walked over to Hudson and placed her hand on his arm. Looking up at Darcy, she reached out her other arm.

Moved by her, he did so without thinking.

With the spirit being the only link between servant and master, the spirit's empathic abilities widened the connection.

Hudson's feelings of loss, despair and heartache moved through her and was pushed into Darcy.

Darcy's body spasmed as he relived every memory that Hudson felt with his mother, culminating in a grand tapestry of grief made from the great departure at the end of all fates.

Overwhelmed by the bond that was now forged between his butler and himself, through the empathic spirit, he fell to the floor, in the same position as Hudson did.

"Hudson," Darcy cried, "I am so sorry. So sorry for everything."

He dug his face into the bed as well, to hide his sorrow. For as he experienced Hudson's loss, he was reminded of his mother's.

Eventually, he looked back at his broken butler and whispered.

"At least you got to see her one last time," Darcy uttered. "At least you said goodbye. In the manner which I was never given."

Turning to the spirit, Darcy began to feel tears swelling up in his eyes.

"I never got to say goodbye."

Gradually, the letters on the ghost's face changed again to reveal one word:

TRUTH

With tender care, Christmas Yet to Come wrapped her arms around Darcy, cradling him like that of a child.

As she did so, he closed his eyes, taking comfort in her kindness, the pages from her gown grew into a cocoon, covering them both as they faded into dark.

CHAPTER 14

The Last of The Spirits

When Darcy opened his eyes, he was alone.

And, in many ways, he was nowhere.

All around him was black. He was standing on something, but it was so dark that he could see neither below him nor what was above.

Just this omnipresent environment of nothing.

"Spirit!" he cried. "Where are you?"

He got no answer.

"Am I to fade into nothing? Am I to be lost? Spirit!"

Once more, he got no response.

Holding his hands together, desperately, he looked back and forth. "I do not deny that I have made many errors, but to be abandoned after I have learned and acquired so much. Please, do not leave me alone."

While he looked into the black, he felt a scene appear behind him.

When he turned, he was not in Hudson's home, or his own townhouse in London.

He was back home in the North, at Pemberley.

There were servants rushing back and forth around him, wondering when Mr. Darcy would return.

At first, Darcy wondered about what he ought to expect, when he realized that some of the servants looked at lot younger than they presently do.

"We're not in the future anymore," he deduced. "*When* are we?"

The housekeeper, Mrs. Reynolds, rushed down the steps that led to the second floor.

"Mrs. Reynolds!" Darcy uttered. He noticed that her hair was not gray, but the blonde hair that he remembered her having when he was in his teens.

Another servant, named Lucy, rushed up to her.

"Where is the master?" Reynolds asked, hurriedly, "Mrs. Darcy will not last the hour if he does not come quickly."

"Tom just saw him riding across the grounds, frantically. He worried his horse might slip into a rabbit hole."

"Even if so, the master would limp here, all the same."

There were loud sounds that came from downstairs. A door burst open and there were harsh and rushed footsteps that raced up the stairs.

Darcy rushed forward to see what desperate soul it was, and his eyes widened, in excitement and joy.

"Father!" Darcy exclaimed.

Mr. Darcy Sr. was dashing up the steps, two at a time, while Mrs. Reynolds met him on the landing.

"How is she?" Darcy Sr. asked, hoarsely, joining Reynolds as they made their way to his wife's bedroom. Lucy trailed behind.

"Doctor Mason is still in her room, but he has—"

Reynolds trailed off heavily, "he said that he regrets that Master Darcy and Miss Darcy are away from home."

Darcy Sr. stopped in his tracks and looked at Reynolds. Horror stricken.

He understood the implications and continued walking to his wife's bedroom.

A bedroom that had become her sickroom for the last month at least.

When he reached her bedroom door, Darcy Sr. halted and froze.

His son had been following him ever since he had come in, awestruck at seeing his father again.

To see the man who raised him to be so fragile in look and so weak, reminded Darcy of when Mr. Hudson had halted at his front door when he heard that his mother was dying.

Seeing both men so frightened of what lay on the other side of the door gave a powerful connection about how similar a master to a large estate can be to a butler who keeps order of things.

At the end of the day, how far apart are we?

Even by nation, by flag, by race, by gender, by identity, how far apart are we?

Only very much by ignorance.

Yet never very much in actuality.

"Papa," Darcy said to his father's back. "She's dying, isn't she? Mama is dying."

His father jerked and jolted back, turning around to look at who just spoke.

Recognizing it, Darcy's eyes widened in astonishment.

"Do you see me?" Darcy asked, stepping forward, overcome. "Father, I am here."

Mr. Darcy Sr. blinked, assuming he had heard nothing, and turned back to the door.

Seeing that his father no longer could look through the veil, Darcy waited.

At last, Darcy's father opened the door, and both men entered.

When father and son walked through, both men had the same expression.

For one was watching his wife pass *away*.

And the one was seeing his mother fading *away*.

"Anne!" Darcy's father uttered, bereft at seeing his wife so weak and barely responsive as she lay in bed. The doctor watched over her.

"Mother!" Darcy cried, for now he was seeing her leave this life, which he had not done before.

Both men rushed to her bedside, with Darcy on the right, and his father on the left.

"Anne." Darcy's father's voice wavered. "How can I bear it! No, I cannot!"

"I'm sorry, sir," the doctor declared. "I have done everything. Yet, it cannot be long now."

Darcy's father ignored the doctor because he was well aware.

He had been in denial, assuming his wife would regain her strength, but her health had declined rapidly, which led to him not calling his children back home in time to give the last farewells. His son was still at university and Georgiana was at Matlock, as a companion to another girl who was a distant cousin who was staying there.

Darcy's father was proven wrong, and he would feel the effects of that mistake for the rest of his life.

But as for Darcy himself—despite being happy to see his father again, his attention was solely on his mother.

For now, he got the chance that he was never given before; he could say goodbye.

"Mother," Darcy whispered, "I know that I'm far away, but I am also here. I'm here."

Darcy received no reply, of course. Yet, he did not need one. He was just happy to have been given one last moment with her before the end had come.

"Anne, dearest," Darcy's father asserted again, "I should have called the children home. God forgive me! Please, fight on."

Even through the weakness, Anne Darcy managed to open her eyes. Her breathing was heavy, and she was having a hard time staying conscious, but she fought on.

"Lionel," Darcy's mother whispered, "I…"

"Don't talk," he insisted. "Please, save your strength."

"There is—no point. I so deeply," she began to weep, "I will miss you."

"And I will miss you! I will miss you so much."

"And the children. Tell them that I love them."

"I will, of course. Forgive me, Anne, I should have sent for them."

"I prefer them to remember me as I was. Not like this."

"I will make sure that they grow up to be everything

that you raised them to be. I will raise them to be as wonderful as you have."

"I know," she said, touching his face. "But Lionel, I must..."

"What?"

"This is important. I..."

"Yes."

"Was wrong. I was wrong, dearest."

"About what?" Darcy Sr. questioned.

"I meant well. After all, every mother wants the best for our children."

"As we ought to. You've made a great road for them."

"And that is where I worry. I want them to be all that we hoped they'd be. But I'd also want them to be happy. I thought that, over time, Fitzwilliam and his cousin would grow to feel a fondness for each other. Catherine and I wanted the best for them, but I wonder—I don't think that they would be suitable for each other."

"They are young; they have yet time."

"Their tempers are too different. I do not think anything like marital joy would find them. Maybe I was wrong to push my will on what is his right to do. Maybe I should have given my son something else, rather than telling him to walk down another person's path. It was my choice, but *not* his. Tell him to be prudent, but his duty does not matter as to what he desires for his love."

She held her husband's hand.

"He and Georgiana—they deserve what we have here. What we have now." She looked deeply into her husband's eyes, "Lionel, I love you, and I regret—"

She did not finish her sentence. Her eyes closed and her

husband wept into the pillow next to her, losing the love of his life.

Between his grief and his wonder Darcy could not believe it!

At the end of her life, his mother spent her last breath going back on every dream she had, for her son's happiness.

All his time with his mother, she had an express wish: for him and Anne de Bourgh, her namesake, to marry.

For the uniting of Pemberley and Rosings Park to become a reality, an empire that would be distinguished among the English aristocracy.

Only for, in her last moment, to go back on her dream and want his happiness more. She wanted him to find a deep love that could be the making of him.

And she used her last seconds to give him that message.

A message that he never received.

The scene dissolved around him, leaving Darcy to wonder about what he had just heard.

A whirlwind of sensations burst through him as he sat there.

At first, it was astonishment.

Next it was wonder.

Afterwards it was confusion.

Lastly, it was anger.

Duty, to a path that he initially held down as law, a path that did neither party any good, had become meaningless.

There was neither rhyme nor reason for what he had given up, for the sake of making others happy.

He looked at his mother's deathbed and barely moved.

All that time wasted, he had a hard time in accepting, in confronting and reconciling it to his present state.

What was it all for?

What was any of it all for?

He cursed silently, bitter.

Suddenly, he heard a piano playing from the music room.

Darcy was not alarmed at the sudden melody that had begun.

At this point, very little in life could shock him now.

Despite that the night was long, and he had been taken on a tumultuous ride through his past, present and future, he still had the energy to move to the next tableau.

He stood and walked to the music room in Pemberley. His feet were heavy, his mind was heavier, and his heart was heaviest.

But he had come so far that he had to go the extra mile that would help it all come together.

When he entered, he saw a familiar face sitting there, playing masterfully on the pianoforte.

Walking up to the bench, he sat down and watched her hands as they glided across the piano keys.

"Hullo, mother," he said.

Anne Darcy's ghost was the woman who was playing on the pianoforte.

"Good morning, son," she responded. "You saw my last moments."

"Yes."

"Are you angry?" she asked.

"Yes."

"Good," she responded, still playing. This surprised her son.

"What?"

"You've lost much because of my dreams, and how I drowned you in them."

"I do not hate you," he assured her.

"I appreciate that."

Darcy sighed.

"You are my mother, who cared for me and loved me. You have no choice but to be the best of women, in my eyes. You spent your last breath trying to make up for the mistake you now call it. Father never told me, which angers me. Father never told me."

"He thought that, in my last moments, I was being sentimental—delusional."

"He thought you didn't mean it? That you were not in earnest?"

"No. He spent so many years hearing my sister and I mention that you and your cousin were perfect for each other. That you were each other's destiny. It was a mistake. A great one, and, while we attempted to make you both, we unmade you both. And he eventually grew to believe it. Thus, all that I can do now is regret."

She continued to play until he placed his hands on hers, forcing her to stop.

"I can touch you now," he observed.

"Yes, you now can."

She placed her hand over his.

"Still love me, through it all?" she asked.

"Even through it all, and because of it all," Darcy assured her. "You always wanted what was best for me, even until the bitter end. My initial reaction was anger." His voice softened. "But why would I be so foolish as to cling to it?"

He wrapped his arm around her, and she pressed herself against him.

"Can we just sit like this, for a little while longer?" Darcy asked. "That's all that I ask."

"And all that I cherish giving."

They remained seated like that, as mother and son.

After a few minutes, of them enjoying being reunited again, Darcy understood that his time grew short.

"Mama," he said, "I need advice now."

"On what to do next?"

"Yes," he said, "I know what I must do, but I'm scared to do it, because I don't know how to do it."

"But what must be done cannot be done too quickly," she added. "You are afraid of seeing Elizabeth Bennet again."

"Yes, I am."

"And you worry that, no matter what you do, or what

you say, she will be angry with you? That everything you say will come out all wrong. And she will want none of you."

"Precisely."

She held his hand.

"Then you have to forgive her and understand the reason for her anger," she said, "when she inevitably gets angry with you for the choice that was never made. For you falling in love with her, and nothing being done over it, and for so long. You must understand that the right path is not the easiest way to go often. It's going to be hard on you, but you must keep trying. Keep believing that she will forgive you for all that has been. Do not abandon her, now, after she has felt the pangs of being abandoned before."

"But what if she no longer loves me?"

"You can only find out if you speak to her."

"And Bingley…?"

"I offer the same advice. Try, my son. The right to try is your main attribute."

"Like I admitted… I am scared."

"So do all those who must apologize for their mistakes. The trick is to use the fear to make you find a better way."

She brushed her hand against his brow.

"The storm is over, my dear boy. Time to look for the light."

"We part ways soon, don't we?" he asked.

"Yes, but I will never fully leave you. Not really. And I shall always love you."

Darcy kissed her forehead.

"And you will always be in my heart."

Anne Darcy smiled.

"I am prodigiously proud of you," she assured him. "And now you know what so much of humanity has learned: the past has already been, and it cannot be re-written or altered. It happened. Do not attempt to change it. The future is yet to come, but the present! Ah, Fitzwilliam, the present! It is out there, waiting for you. Chase it, son. Chase it!

There was a blinding light, which made Darcy shut his eyes.

CHAPTER 15
Redemption

When Darcy opened his eyes, he jerked forward.

"Where am I?" he asked. Squinting, he looked around and found himself in his sitting room, in his armchair, where he had dozed.

When seeing that he was safe, and back in his parlor, from the night before, where he had first been disturbed by the spirits, he breathed a sigh of relief.

Though, in truth, the sigh of relief was the last to come.

At first, he was confused.

And discombobulated.

Next, he looked around to see if another spirit would appear.

Then he looked at the nearest window and saw some light coming through it.

The night was over.

The dawn was calling out to him.

That was when he felt relief.

Still sitting in his chair, he closed his eyes, letting the events of the evening's encounters wash over him.

"I'm home," he said with a sigh, "I'm not certain what day it is, but I'm home. I feel it, Mother, I feel that I have been returned at the proper time. Unless it didn't happen."

He stood up, began pacing back and forth, being tossed between facts and faith. Between doubt and dreams. Between logic over lost loves.

"Perhaps it never did," he uttered, "yet it felt real. Dreams can easily feel as such. As do nightmares. Nothing could have easily happened at all. And I was merely—"

He cut himself off when he turned to the piano.

The very piano that his mother was playing at before.

Slowly, he walked up to it, reached out and ran his hand along the keys.

A thousand sensations came upon him, as he recalled every moment that he had with her. And all the many occurrences that followed.

"But it did," he whispered to himself, "and even if it didn't, what does it matter?"

He placed his arms over the front of the piano, leaned forward and rested his face on the back of his palms.

"Mother," he uttered, with his eyes closed, "thank you. Thank you for everything. I know it now, more than ever, that it's never too late. I can begin again. Everything has a right to start anew if the intention is pure and there is yet time. Time, I do have. I have all the time in the world!" He chuckled. "All the time in the world."

❧

From outside of the parlor, he heard footsteps.

For a fleeting moment, he wondered if it was his mother's ghost, or one of the Christmas Spirits.

Yet, the other world was gone, and he was within the realm of the living as Mr. Jefferson entered.

"Sir," Jefferson asked, "good morning."

When seeing him, Darcy's eyes lit up slightly. Not too much, because even though the transformation had been complete, and he was a better man now, he still was Mr. Darcy. As such, expressions would not be too large, but gradual and more contained. Yet, everything he felt was sincere and true, through it all.

"I noticed that your bed was already made up after I inquired after you, upstairs. Did you, perhaps, fall asleep by the fire in here?"

"Yes," Darcy said. "I do believe that I did. Jefferson?"

"Yes."

"What day is it?"

Jefferson looked confused.

"What day is it?" Jefferson repeated.

"Yes."

"Well, it's Christmas Day, sir."

Darcy's eyes widened.

"Christmas Day?"

"Yes, sir."

Astounded, Darcy looked back at the pianoforte and of the books along the walls.

"It was all done in one night," he said to himself, "all of it."

Jefferson watched his master. Even though Darcy was a

cold man, Jefferson still had come to feel for what he called a 'broken soul'.

"Sir, are you quite well?" Jefferson questioned, worried that his master had gone a little mad. "Should I send for a doctor?"

"No," Darcy said, standing up quicker than normal. This did not escape his manservant. "No, I am quite well, thank you. It just occurred to me that you will have a very busy day."

"Well, yes. I am aware that since the rest of the servants have been given the day, I will oversee everything."

"No, that is not what I mean. Jefferson, I am terribly sorry that I have given you such last-minute notice on all these things. But it cannot he helped. Follow me."

Jefferson followed Darcy up the steps, who *now* began to develop a natural energy, especially after it was sparked from having much to set right.

"First," Darcy began, "I have to go to Bingley's residence and speak to him immediately."

"Mr. Bingley's home?"

"Yes. I must do a very hard thing, but what must be done cannot be done too quickly. He will not wish to see me, but it cannot be helped."

He entered his bedroom.

"I do not need you to warm up water for a bath. Just boil some water and I shall take a quick sponge bath. While you do that, can you lay out my best clothes for the occasion?"

"Yes, I can."

"Afterwards, I am going to Colonel Fitzwilliam's for the dinner party."

Jefferson said nothing, but Darcy sensed his surprise.

"It is not too indecorous and irrational, is it?" Darcy asked him. "To arrive, despite having declined the invitation? We are family, after all, and I trust that my cousin would forgive me."

'I am quite certain that he would," Jefferson said, with a lighter tone from being given some good news for a change. "Quite so. Quite so, I believe. He would be glad to see you, especially now that he is soon to be married. If it is not too bold of me to point out."

"It is not too bold."

"His fiancée is Miss Catherine Bennet, from Hertfordshire, correct?"

"Yes, she is."

"Then perhaps, most of her family will be there to celebrate."

Darcy half-smiled.

"You hit the nail right on the head, Jefferson. I know that they will be."

Jefferson suppressed a chuckle.

Once he finished getting the clothes assembled, he mentioned that he would go down and boil some water.

"Thank you," Darcy said, warmly. "Also, when I finish this letter, can you have it sent posthaste tomorrow. It has a long way to go, and I want it to arrive as soon as possible."

"A letter to Scotland?"

"No. New York, of our old American colonies. I'm writing to my sister, asking if I can come and visit her."

When hearing that, Jefferson's shoulders relaxed, and his eyes were filled with wonder and excitement, but it was a subtle sort of thing. To be a proper manservant, it was never courteous to display much emotion. He was exhilarated, but it was in a quiet sort of way.

"Of, course, sir," Jefferson said, his tone casual, but warm. "I very much shall see to it personally."

"Good man," Darcy said, still writing.

Jefferson walked to the doorway and then turned around.

"Sir, forgive me, but I have to ask."

"Yes?"

"Has something happened?"

Putting down his pen, Darcy looked at his lap and rubbed his hands together.

"A lot has, but in a very unspeakable sort of way," he explained, "you do not need to trouble yourself on that account. But I just discovered something that it took me too long to learn." He looked at Jefferson. "I'm an idiot."

Jefferson could not control the look of surprise and amusement on his face.

"Oh."

"Yes," Darcy said, a chuckle escaping him. "I just learned that I am an idiot."

"Oh well then," Jefferson interjected, "never fear. That is a lesson that we all learn, usually later than earlier."

"Yes. And I appreciate that you tried to apply that revelation into a general one that all humanity shares. Now I feel less alone."

"I thought it would be the correct thing, and you are most welcome. Permission to say Merry Christmas?"

"Of course. Merry Christmas, Jefferson, merrier a Christmas than I have ever given before."

"Thank you."

Jefferson went off to prepare his master's water.

As he did so, Darcy went back to his letter to his younger sister.

"So many words to say," Darcy uttered to the paper, "now to say all of them."

He continued writing.

Once he was dressed, it was the time of atonement.

Darcy, along with Jefferson, traveled to Bingley's home.

"I do believe that he is at home," Darcy said to Jefferson, "During Christmas day, he also preferred to sleep in, having gone to mass on Christmas Eve. Hopefully, nothing has changed."

"I believe so," Jefferson said, "I recall Master Bingley always being a creature of habit."

They knocked on the door, asked if the master was home, and they were informed that he was not at home.

But Darcy knew what that meant; Bingley was at home, but he simply did not wish to see him.

"Please," Darcy issued to the butler, "Ask your master again, and inform him that I have very important information, regarding a certain lady from his past, from Hertfordshire."

The butler did as he was instructed, and soon returned, granting him entry.

Darcy was shown into the drawing room, while Jefferson was shown downstairs, to the kitchens where he could warm himself and be given some chocolate to drink.

While Darcy waited, looking out at the window, he

watched children in the street, who were sliding down the road by hanging on the back of carriages.

Someone entered the room, and he knew that it was Bingley.

"Remember," Darcy said, "when you were a child, and you got into all sorts of mischief when it was snowing?"

"Yes," Bingley responded. "I do."

His voice was restrained and calm, missing its traditional cheer.

"Sadly, I do not," Darcy responded. "Being a Darcy, I was unable to do the many things those other children did. Yet, I wish I had. Things might have been different."

"I suppose so," Bingley responded. "Am I allowed to say Merry Christmas to you?"

"You may. And I shall in return."

"Merry Christmas."

"And Merry Christmas to you as well."

Bingley walked up to Darcy.

"Darcy, why have you come?"

"For your welfare. And for mine. I'm sorry."

Bingley blinked.

"For what? You say that you are sorry? For what, precisely?"

"Everything."

At first, Bingley said nothing, because he was a little speechless. At last, he found his voice.

"Darcy, you must understand that this is not easy for me."

"Nor I."

"I know. I appreciate that you have realized this, but it still does not change things."

"And it ought not to. I have made many mistakes over the last few years. Our friendship's ending was among those."

"You admit that you were in the wrong?"

"Totally and completely."

Bingley still did not look at him.

"Still, Darcy it is not as easy as that. You said that you came here regarding a lady from Hertfordshire."

"Yes, I did."

Bingley breathed in heavily.

"Is it about Miss Jane Bennet?"

"Yes."

Bingley closed his eyes.

"What has happened to her? I am braced for hard news."

"Nothing hard," Darcy responded, realizing that he had not been very forthcoming. "Forgive me, I did not mean to make you believe the worst."

"What was I to believe?! You look graver than ever."

"That's just how my face is."

Bingley rolled his eyes.

"True. I had forgotten."

"Quite frankly, I cannot see how."

Despite their estrangement, both men did chuckle at that. Soon, it quieted down.

"Tell me then," Bingley continued, "what of Miss Bennet? At this point, it is of little matter, but I shall like to know all the same."

"Tonight, I am going to my cousin's dinner party. The Colonel's. The party's intention is plural. It's to celebrate the holiday, and his engagement, to Miss Catherine Bennet."

When hearing that, Bingley's eyes widened as he forgot any resentment and gave way to curiosity.

"Colonel Fitzwilliam is marrying Miss Kitty?"

"Yes."

"What happened? Did one of them suddenly come into wealth?"

"Richard did. One of his uncles on his mother's side, Uncle Marley, passed away without an heir. He left everything to Richard, who now has retired his commission and is going into politics. Once he achieves his new life, he's done what he's always wanted to do."

"What was that?"

"Be able to marry where he wishes and without considering the woman's dowry."

"He's been in love with Jane's—" he cut himself off, to correct himself. "He's been in love with Miss Bennet's little sister for all this time?"

"Very much so, it appears."

Bingley chuckled sadly.

"Well, the Colonel is much braver than you and I, is he not? To marry as he wants."

"There's more."

"What more? What worse?"

"More, but not worse. Of course, her sisters will be in attendance. As will the two eldest, who are recently unattached. Miss Elizabeth has become widowed over this last year and Miss Bennet never married."

When hearing this, Bingley's whole posture changed. He turned to Darcy, with a jerk.

"Never married? When I had last spoken to Caroline on the matter, she said that Miss Bennet was courting someone and that they were soon to wed."

"She was partly correct. Miss Bennet was in a courtship, but she did not marry the man. I am quite certain that Miss Bingley assumed it, for quite a few reasons. But I can assure you that she never married. I've…"

Darcy trailed off as he wondered the best way to go about it.

"I know that you must already have a prior engagement, however, I was wondering if you would come with me to the party. We could begin to reacquaint ourselves with the Bennets again. As well as atone for the mistake that was made long ago."

"The mistake?" Bingley responded. "The mistake that I made for listening to you and my sisters."

"If you are worried about how you shall be viewed," Darcy added, "then I will acknowledge my entire explanation. I will take all the blame on myself."

Bingley looked away from him and sat down, disturbed.

"Bingley," Darcy began gently, "I know that you are angry with me, and you have every right to be. I acted wrongly and perhaps allowed my own misery to cloud my judgment. I have no facts that Miss Bennet was indifferent to you. All that I had were blind assumptions, and again, I apologize. But I'm here now, attempting to set things on the right course. What say you?"

Bingley sighed.

"She will hate seeing me. They will hate seeing the both of us."

"I know. But that is a risk that I am willing to take to correct what I have done."

"It's been so many years. Miss Bennet probably does not even care for me any longer. And she would be right to."

"As Miss Elizabeth ought not to care for me, but I must try. We owe them that much."

Bingley leaned back in his chair.

"It was not just you that I despised," he continued, "yes, you pressured me. As did my sisters. But I also allowed myself to be persuaded."

Bingley rubbed his eyes and continued.

"I was angry with myself for being weak and not following my own heart. After all, what was in there was real."

"It was not easy," Darcy said, "I was very convincing."

"But I should have been stronger, and now here my life is. I fear her hating me."

"If she does, then give her time. Try again, as I am about to." Realizing that he was unprepared for this sort of reaction, Darcy attempted to find the best way to convince his friend to try again. Only for, in the next second, for him to see what Bingley was afraid of happening.

"You're afraid of the dream," Darcy determined.

"Dream?" Bingley asked.

"It's been years since you've seen Miss Bennet, and that was enough to put her on a pedestal. She has become the ultimate dream, hasn't she? As a result, there's no way that dream could happen. It's only in here," Darcy said, pointing to his head. "And if you see Miss Bennet again, you either are afraid that the present will not live up to the dreams of her from the past. Or that you will disappoint her. Or am I wrong?"

Bingley leaned forward and looked at the flames that flickered in the fireplace.

"How could you possibly know that?" Bingley asked. "I barely know of it, myself."

"Because it's what I have been feeling, and I had an impulse that we were the same in our imagination as well as in our history. We're two men who fell in love with two sisters, at the same time, and let them go at the same time. I had an inkling, made a guess, and I am happy to be correct."

"Why does that make you happy?"

"Because now your predicament is an ailment that I can treat." Darcy sat down, opposite Bingley and faced him. "When we walked into Hertfordshire, we were walking into a fairytale. Then we walked away from it, and now all we have is reality. But that's also how every marriage starts and ends."

Darcy walked over to the decanter, poured Bingley some brandy and handed it to him.

"Fairytale first, reality last. That's how life unfolds. But that does not stop it from being anything less than beautiful. Will the Bennet sisters hate us when we return into their lives? Yes, perhaps they might. And they have every right to. As it is our correct *duty* to give them time to accept us. We're walking into a reality, a harsh and bitter reality that we gave them. Therefore, how about we attempt to give them a bit of the fairytale that we have left in us?"

"I fear that if I go, and she has no love for me at all, I shall die."

"Believe me, you are *not* going to die."

Bingley chuckled sadly at this.

"I suppose there is nothing for it," Bingley said, "I'll just go to a dinner party that I am terrified of."

"I as well. Haven't I given you a wonderful Christmas present?"

"Yes, Darcy, I owe you for this, and will pay you back, in full, if it proves emotionally fatal."

"Appreciate it."

CHAPTER 16
Reality Turned Fairytale

C hristmas day will always have a warmness to the event, and all around, Darcy felt the joy and merriment that the city was abuzz with.

He heard the Chimes of Midnight.

On every wall, it was as if he saw happy words written along people's cheeks.

And finally, he heard the music of the city.

At last, he arrived at Colonel Fitzwilliam's residence. The party was already underway, guests could be seen from the window, and animated voices came from within.

"I feel like I am about to faint," Bingley said.

"Never fear," Darcy said, "I'm good at catching things."

Both men knocked on the door, informed the butler that they were expected, and they entered to see people rushing round the room, because games were being played.

One woman was in the center, her eyes blindfolded, as she tried to move around and catch someone.

It was Jane Bennet.

When Bingley saw her, as beautiful as ever, smiling and

clearly still letting her bloom cling about her, he forgot himself.

Instinctively, he walked towards her.

Everyone in the party froze, seeing him slowly make his way in her direction. The room grew suddenly silent. After all, some people knew the history between these two.

"What happened?" Jane laughed. "It's like the room is empty. You all didn't leave, did you? Because that would be most unfair. And if you are playing a trick on me by you all being quiet, I'll still catch you. Because when you move, I'll hear it."

Jane continued to walk forward; her arms stretched out.

And Bingley stood there.

She got closer, reached out and touched his nose.

"Found someone!" Jane cried. Gradually she moved her hands all over Bingley's face and neck. He just stood there, all too glad to have her hands on his skin.

He smiled, despite what could happen.

"Well," Jane said, still trying to decide on who it was. "I admit that I am a poor judge at these sorts of things." She laughed. "I shall guess that it is you, Mr. Topper."

She removed the blindfold, grinning as she assumed that she would be correct.

Therefore, imagine her surprise when she saw a familiar face, that she thought she would never see again.

There Jane and Bingley were, staring at each other, with their faces quite close.

"Merry Christmas, Miss Bennet," Bingley whispered, breathy.

"Mr. Bingley!" Jane responded.

And then she fainted.

~

As Jane Bennet collapsed, Bingley caught her.

Instinctively, Darcy rushed in to assist him, but he was not alone with that inclination.

A younger sister rushed to her older sister and held her waist as Bingley still propped her up.

Since both lunged forward, to help, they almost collided into each other, equally astonished.

"Mr. Darcy!" Elizabeth cried.

"Miss Elizabeth!" Darcy responded.

All they could do was stare at each other. At first, but then Elizabeth could not resist saying something.

"Never fear catching me," she said, "I am against fainting."

"Ah," he said, quickly falling back into the tenderness that he once felt for her. "I was of the notion that would be so."

"Yes."

Colonel Fitzwilliam stepped forward.

"Darcy?" Colonel Fitzwilliam asked.

"Merry Christmas, cousin. I've—I've come to dinner."

"Clearly," Colonel Fitzwilliam said, raising an eyebrow.

"If you will have me," Darcy finished.

Colonel Fitzwilliam smiled.

"Bingley," Kitty said, going up to him, "bring my sister to the other room. I have some smelling salts in there to revive her."

Bingley carried Jane Bennet to the other room, where Kitty followed her.

"I should come as well," Elizabeth responded.

"Would you be needing any assistance?" Darcy asked.

She gave him a cold look.

"I think I can manage."

"Of course," Darcy responded. In truth, that was the best that he could hope for.

Outside of those seeing to Jane, Colonel Fitzwilliam turned to his cousin.

"You really mean to come to dinner?" he asked.

"Yes."

"And to be pleasant and not a taciturn and disagreeable fellow."

"Yes. I should have come sooner, much sooner. But may I come?"

Colonel Fitzwilliam laughed and clapped him on the shoulder.

"Of, course!" he cried. "Yes, of course!"

Everyone in the crowd agreed with equal fervor.

The people swarmed around him.

Among them was the Fitzwilliam family, including Mary and Mr. Collins, and Lydia Denny, along with her husband.

"Mr. Darcy and Mr. Bingley are back!" Lydia laughed. "What a good joke!"

"Less of a joke," Mary said, "and more of a miracle."

"Yes," Mr. Collins said, "for at this holy time of year, the good lord can smile on us in incredible ways. Mr. Darcy, we had no idea that we had the honor of your coming."

"To confess it," Darcy said, "I had no notion of my coming until this morning. And a good idea that it was to have. I was hoping that I would be welcome. I appreciate your kindness. And I hope that you can find a spot for me at dinner."

"Of course," Colonel Fitzwilliam said.

Lord and Lady Fitzwilliam greeted him as well, and all the other guests were quick to accost him, in a lively mood.

Anne de Bourgh had been unable to attend, because her health was not the best and she had a sore throat, leaving her unable to travel. Darcy was inwardly relieved because he knew that he needed more time before he faced her again. Besides, it was as he recalled the Ghost of Christmas Present showing him.

Darcy quickly fell into the rhythm of being social, especially since people were used to avoiding him. And to know that this time, they were welcome, was food to a starving man.

However, there was one face that he had to see—rather, that he *needed* to see. Or he would go mad.

After a while, he untangled himself from the group, walking to the room that Jane was recovering in. With Bingley being in the room, along with two of her sisters, Darcy felt that he could proceed safely.

He knocked and entered to find Jane fully recovered. Her legs were stretched across a lounge chair, while Bingley crouched down next to her, on the floor and they were wholly engrossed in each other's conversation.

On the other side of the room, were Kitty and Elizabeth. Since a chaperone was needed, they thought it was best to remain. However, when they saw Darcy enter, Kitty gave Elizabeth a knowing look.

Elizabeth nodded to her, indicating that it was suitable for her to leave them alone together.

Kitty excused herself and walked to the doorway, passing Darcy in the process.

As she did so, she stopped to have a few words with him.

"Well, you surprised us," Kitty announced.

"I surprised myself." He looked down at her. "We are about to be cousins, aren't we?"

"Yes."

"I am happy for you and for Richard. He loves you very much."

"And I love him. I think I must be the most fortunate woman in England. Not many women get the chance to marry the man they love, and for him to be a good man at that."

"This is the time of the year for it, I daresay?"

"Yes. Wonderful."

Kitty leaned forward, lowering her voice even more.

"Elizabeth is looking very well, is she not?"

"Yes," Darcy answered, looking over her shoulder at her older sister. "She always looks well."

"Do not hurt her," Kitty asserted, suddenly serious. Darcy turned to her and was surprised to see a unique ferocity in her eye. "Do not *hurt* her."

All Darcy could do was nod.

"Good man," Kitty said, "now excuse me, I have a fiancé to not leave alone with his guests."

She left the room, leaving the two 'couples' alone.

Now was the moment of insecurity.

It was time to face the woman who he had abandoned to a duty that was fruitless to achieve.

He was not like Bingley, who knew how to ingratiate himself into a situation very quickly, even if he wronged the person he talked to.

Even though Darcy had to convince him to come, Bingley knew how to begin.

Darcy was eager to come but did not know how to start.

Bingley and Jane looked at Darcy, took a quick look at Lizzy, and then looked away, continuing to talk.

That left Elizabeth and Darcy to gaze at each other, apprehensively.

It would be lovely for them to look at one another, fall in love instantly, and all would be forgiven and forgotten.

Yet, Darcy knew that the fairytale still rested in Hertfordshire, years ago, and reality in London was what must be faced.

In his eyes there was supplication and a sense of defeat. He wanted Elizabeth to understand that he felt such remorse.

She was able to perceive, because when looking into his eyes, she gestured for him to sit next to him.

Overjoyed at the invitation, despite being unaware of what would follow, he approached her slowly and sat down next to her.

"It is a pleasure to see you again."

Elizabeth smiled gently, and she tapped her lap, contemplative.

"It is unique to see you here. But I shall be frank and admit that I cannot say seeing you again is a pleasure.

Despise me if you dare, but as you know, I am not afraid of you."

"And I would not have you so." Darcy looked ahead, rather than at her, to make it easier on them both. "You have just cause to be angry with me."

"Indeed, I do," she answered strongly.

When hearing her pertinent remark, it had the opposite effect rather than draw him away. In fact, it lured him in, because now they could get to the heart of the matter.

"Still saucy as ever," Darcy responded.

"Still unafraid. Besides, my sauciness savors strongly of justice." Elizabeth began to fan herself because she knew that her spirit was rising. "Besides, you are no liar and prefer to hear the absolute truth on things. Whether you like it or not, I am a truth. And I cannot be denied."

"No, you cannot be."

"Mr. Darcy, look at me."

He did not.

"Why do you fear my face?" she pursued.

"I am mortified, is all. You try looking into the face of a woman that you hurt, wrongfully, and that you have much to atone for."

"I loved my husband," Elizabeth said, "if that helps you. Our marriage was an adventure, and it helped me learn and grow through our match. Despite my anger for you abandoning me, I do not regret my marriage with him."

"I am sorry for your loss. He must've been a good man to have secured your respect and affection."

"Thank you for offering your condolences," Elizabeth

said, "but I do not think that you were happy for me marrying at all."

Darcy looked at her sharply, she raised her eyebrows and again, saw right through him.

"You hated the idea of me being married," she declared. "Tell me that the wicked side of you does not see that I am right."

Darcy sighed.

"Very well. You are correct. I hated your husband. Even though I never met him during my life, I wished that you and he had never met."

Elizabeth chuckled.

"I had an inkling. First, he was the best man I could have found, after I lost you, so he deserves your respect. And second, your theory was that, if we did not marry, then I could marry no one."

"As irrational as that sounds, yes."

"Well, that is a delicious sort of revenge that I am very happy for."

Darcy looked at her, unafraid now. Again, he was drawn in, because Elizabeth did not fear making the hair on his hands stand on end. Her bold and fearless remarks always drew him in.

He crossed his legs, shifted his body more in her direction and placed his arm over the back of the sofa, in a more comfortable manner.

"What revenge did it invoke, pray tell?" he asked her, intrigued.

Elizabeth turned more towards him, rather than forward, challengingly.

"You were the love of my life, and then you abandoned all pursuit of me. I hated you. There were days and nights that I dreamed of clawing your eyes out. I wished that you would get thrown from a horse. I hoped no woman would ever stoop to love your insufferable soul. I envisioned many ways in which you could be hurt and suffer greatly. Oh, Mr. Darcy! I found so much satisfaction in those musings."

"I am certain that it brought a grander sparkle to your eyes."

"It did. It did." Elizabeth chuckled a little and Darcy smiled. "Then I found love again, and it was brilliant. It was like you didn't exist in my heart."

"That's a bold lie; you were still in love with me."

"Stop interrupting. It vexes me." Darcy kept quiet and Lizzy continued. "And then, after learning that the reason that you forsook me, was to marry your cousin, out of a strange obligation from an arranged marriage that your mothers planned. Only for that marriage to NEVER happen because your cousin rejected you. And the reason why was because your cousin embraced that delightful thing called 'common sense', which you lacked in every respect. So, all your foolish intentions came to nothing, and you threw me over, for a fate that never came."

Elizabeth smiled at him, wickedly.

"*That*, Mr. Darcy, was my favorite part. But if that was not comfort enough to me, I kept hearing about how you fell apart, became a classic misanthrope worthy of being in a Moliere play, your sister chose her husband against your expectations, Bingley abandoned you, and your whole life fell apart, with only your wealth to keep you warm at night. Oh, Mr. Darcy, you tortured yourself so much, that I no longer needed to torture you in my mind. It almost makes me giddy."

At this point, they could not take their eyes off each other.

"There," Elizabeth finalized, "I have done. You may speak now."

At this point, Darcy had only one thing to say.

"So… what you're saying is that you're still in love with me."

Elizabeth dropped her face into her palm.

"That's all that you heard from my speech, was it not?"

"Yes," Darcy responded. "If it helps, I am still very much in love with you."

Elizabeth looked at him.

"You are?"

"Yes, Miss Bennet. Oh, forgive me, I must stop calling you that."

"You may call me Elizabeth," she allowed. When hearing that, Darcy felt elated and even more enthralled. "We are to be cousins, and so, you may call me by my first name as much as you like."

"As you can call me Fitzwilliam."

"No, I cannot."

"Elizabeth!"

"Your first name is part of your family's last name. It's too confusing."

"True. Darcy will do."

"Oh, it always will," Elizabeth said.

Instinctively, Darcy took her hand. Realizing that it was improper, he released it.

Always in a gaming mood, even when she was serious,

Elizabeth looked at him gently. Slowly, she reached out her hand for him to take. Like a drowning man to a raft, he took it and was all too happy when she closed her fingers around his palm.

"You've grown bolder than ever, thank goodness," he responded.

"You hurt me, when you went away," Elizabeth said, serious, "and that hurt rested in me for years."

"As you saw, I broke when I abandoned you. I hurt for very long as well. But I am here now, and if you will have me, I would like to try again."

Elizabeth rolled her head.

"You have a woman with two different inclinations. A part of me wishes to say no, just to torment you more. But another part of me wants to say yes."

"I am heartily sorry for everything. Please, let me make it up to you."

She gave him a side glance.

"Right now, I still am in mourning for my husband. But I am also aware that ignoring one's heart, I have learned, is a foolish and fruitless endeavor. Therefore, I have no choice but to say yes eventually."

Darcy's face lit up, merry.

"You will?"

"Yes, I will. Just give me more time. I have the right to miss him."

He held her hand tighter.

"You have made me so happy. I thought—when I came here, I had no expectations. Hopes, yes. But no expectations. And for you to be this way... how soon do you wish to marry?"

When hearing that, Elizabeth gasped.

"What? Are you insane?"

Elizabeth accidentally spoke so loudly that she interrupted the sweet nothings that Jane and Mr. Bingley were speaking to each other.

"What goes on over there?" Mr. Bingley asked, amused.

Elizabeth addressed all three of them.

"Normally I do not repeat conversations that were intimate, but since the four of us have undergone quite the eccentric journey, I shall break my rule for the moment. Jane and Mr. Bingley, after years of being parted, Mr. Darcy has proposed marriage to me."

"Ah, congratulations!" Jane cried.

"What?" Elizabeth gasped.

"But shan't you?" Bingley asked.

"Not you too."

She turned back to Mr. Darcy.

"An eventual courtship is better; do you not agree?" Elizabeth asked.

"Why?" Darcy asked. "When we are obviously going to marry eventually anyway?"

Elizabeth rubbed her lip.

"We have not seen each other in years, Darcy," she countered, lowering her voice again. "We need time to get to know each other again. I would like us to do this properly."

"But we can get to know each other while we are

married," Darcy repeated, his tone animated. Elizabeth's eyes twinkled as she pinched his fingers.

"Let me have this, please?" she asked.

Darcy sighed.

"Oh, very well. When you deem it the proper time, we can enter a courtship then."

"That would be most agreeable." Elizabeth's tone got even more lively. "Oh, and I forgot to mention. In this courtship, you are not allowed to break it off. Only I have that right."

Darcy cocked his head to the side.

"Truly?"

"Yes, that is the rule that I am setting down, and you would do right to accept it. You wronged me once. You will not do so again. And if one of us breaks it off, it shall be my right, and mine alone. You have no say in the matter. Are we in accord?"

"Yes," Darcy gave in, "I think that we are."

"Good."

Both looked into each other's eyes, and they felt the link they had achieved so long ago, back in Hertfordshire. When it had been a fairytale for them both.

In that moment, they realized that they could find their way back again.

Elizabeth's eyes shifted from amused, to simple, then from simple to serious, and serious to wistfully romantic.

"I missed you, Darcy," she whispered, heartfelt and emotionally.

"And I missed you every day."

"You must not go away again," Elizabeth stressed, "this time, you had better come to stay."

Darcy moved himself almost completely next to her, to the point where their legs were touching.

"I'm here," Darcy assured her, "and I am never leaving you. I'm here to stay when you are ready to have me."

"Good," she replied, almost weeping.

Throwing even more caution to the winds and abandoning what little bit of propriety that they had left, Darcy pressed his forehead against hers.

They sat there like that, for some time, becoming lost in each other's company.

In his heart, Darcy felt the light.

He heard the music.

And the chimes of midnight.

"I will always love you," Darcy stressed.

"And you will always be in my heart."

And thus began the road of the rest of their lives... together.

The door opened and Colonel Fitzwilliam entered.

Bingley and Darcy moved away from the sisters that they loved, straightening their waistcoats.

But it was too late; the Colonel had seen it all.

Smiling, he crossed his arms over his shoulder.

"Nice try, gentlemen," he said, "nice try. I came to announce that it is time for us to go into dinner."

Both gentlemen took each sister's arm, who they fancied, and led them into dinner.

Bingley smiled.

Darcy didn't, but he radiated with happiness.

After all, both men had walked in as a mountain of uncertainty.

Now they walked to the dinner table with joy at knowing their fortune had greatly improved.

As the night progressed, Bingley had accosted Darcy, overjoyed.

"Thank you," Bingley said, "for urging me to come. If I had not, things would not have turned out in such a way."

"I told you that Miss Bennet would have given you another chance."

"I know. And to think, that I almost did not listen. I believe that Miss Bennet still cares for me."

"She does. We have been given a second chance, Bingley. Let's chase it."

"Oh, I intend to."

Darcy smiled.

"As do I."

They both stared at the women that they fancied.

"Let us go to it," Darcy said, "without fear."

Elizabeth and Jane Bennet looked back at the men whose hearts they had not lost, and there was a mutual understanding.

Love had never been lost.

Merely delayed.

"Thank you, Mother," Darcy said, under his breath. "Thank you for everything."

After dinner, Colonel Fitzwilliam and Kitty announced that it was time for dancing.

Mary was all too eager to volunteer to play, and Mr. Collins agreed to turn the pages for her.

This gave Mr. Darcy ample opportunity to do the one thing that he had desired to do.

When choosing his partner, he walked straight to Elizabeth, before anyone else would ask her.

"Cousin Elizabeth," he said, "I am aware that I am not tolerable enough to dance with, but if you would do me the honor of taking my hand, then I would be overjoyed."

Staring deeply into his eyes, Elizabeth took his hand eagerly.

"You've come a long way," she said, "I don't know what caused it, but I can see it in your eyes. You have come far."

"In ways that you cannot imagine."

"Keep going," she encouraged, "I prefer it."

They stood up together, Mary began to play, and the Sir Roger de Coverley dance began.

Through the music and the rhythm, Darcy and Elizabeth found themselves again, in the depth of their eyes and hearts, discovering and rediscovering what made them so united.

And so began the road where they were on the path to true love: by correcting the dance they did not experience when they first met.

They had come full circle.

And so now, they could begin again.

And it could be done right.

That is love for you.

Epilogue

A YEAR LATER...

Through the halls in her home in New York, Georgiana Mayweather was in a state of excitement and anticipation. With every servant she approached, she confirmed if all the rooms were ready, her children were dressed, the house was warm enough and there was a blaze in every fireplace that had an occupant.

"Mr. Mayweather!" she called, going to her husband's library. She knocked and entered to see her husband writing.

"Dearest," she said, "they might be here any minute."

"I'm almost done." He took Georgiana's hand and kissed it. "Georgie, I think I might be nervous."

"Nervous," she said, holding his shoulders. "Why? There are so many of them, that you barely have to do any talking. They will supply it."

"I like that notion, but let's be frank. Your brother never wanted you to marry me."

"That's all done," Georgiana assured him, sitting down in his lap as he wrapped his arms around her. "You've seen the letters that he has sent each month since last Christmas. He has felt such regret over it all, and my brother tells the truth. Besides, now he's a married man and it suits him. He will understand us. And if there's one woman who can make him agreeable to you, it's his wife. He adores her enough to not be anything else but cordial."

There was a knock on the library door, and a servant entered.

"Sir and madam," she said, "your whole family is at the door, Mrs. Mayweather."

Georgiana practically dashed out of the room, pulling her husband along.

When they waited in the drawing room, with their children next to them, the newly arrived guests were shown into the house.

All of them.

First, it was Mary and Mr. Collins.

Next, it was Lydia and Captain Denny.

Afterwards, it was Jane and Mr. Bingley.

Then it was Kitty and Colonel Fitzwilliam.

Next it was Caroline Bingley with her husband.

Also, surprisingly, there was Anne de Bourgh.

And for the last…

It was Mr. Darcy, with Elizabeth.

All married couples, and Anne, entered and it was a merry party indeed. Followed by Jefferson, who was left to ensure everything was handled properly. After which, he was going to be allowed to enjoy a holiday in a new city.

Georgiana was overjoyed, where there were many embraces made, and many repeats of the words 'Merry Christmas'.

Georgiana had finally had her family come to see her, who had travelled across an ocean, to their one-time American colonies that felt foreign, but familiar.

The joys of seeing them all were satisfying enough.

But there was one reconciliation that remained to be the greatest.

At last, Darcy had come forward, with Elizabeth on his arm.

Georgiana faced him, with her husband beside her.

"Brother," Georgiana uttered, "welcome to New York, and back into my life."

"Thank you. My apologies for not being in the party at Easter. I had a woman to convince to love me again. And now I can say that I understand the kind of power of love that you have found. I bring you a sister."

"Yes, you do."

Elizabeth and Georgiana faced each other.

"Sister," Elizabeth said, "I worried this moment would never happen."

"So did I. Finally!"

"I know. Finally! Now, I have a brother-in-law to see."

"Indeed, you do," Georgiana said, "this is my husband, Mr. Mayweather."

He warmly made their acquaintance, and turned to Darcy, who still had not spoken.

"Speak, husband," Elizabeth said, "it's your cue."

"Mr. Mayweather," Darcy began, "I thank you for inviting me. I can see that you have done a splendid job at loving my sister and giving her everything that she deserves."

"She was the making of me," Mr. Mayweather said.

"I can see it, all too plain, after years of being blind. Can you forgive a fool for taking too long to see that you were perfect for each other?"

"This is the time of the year for that. Yes, I can. Welcome to my home, Darcy."

At last, Darcy turned to Georgiana.

"Brother," she began.

"Georgiana," he said, "I have been a terrible older brother for too long. But I'm here now if you will have me be so. I missed you."

"I missed you as well."

Darcy's eyes were fighting back tears. In his sister's face, he saw his mother also staring back at him.

"I wish I had the correct words to apologize for all that I have missed."

"You finally came. That's enough."

Georgiana rushed into his arms, and they embraced.

"Welcome to my home," Georgiana said, as she released him, and Darcy took Elizabeth's hand.

"Yes," Darcy smiled. "Welcome home."

Darcy was better than his word. He did it all, and infinitely more.

He became as good a friend, as good a master, as good a husband, as good a family member, and as good a man as the good old city knew, or any other good old city, town, borough, in the good old world.

He transformed, caring more for his servants, giving them the sufficient amount of days to visit their families, made certain that Mr. Hudson was given the proper amount of time to see to his mother, and to give them a kinder household to run.

To Bingley, they re-established their bond, and it was as if no time had been lost.

To the Bennet family, he abandoned his belief of their 'lack of refinement' and simply found them sincere and charming.

He and his family would visit Hertfordshire, which was the place where their paths had crossed.

Also, he and Anne de Bourgh did reconcile, for she still was determined to rule her life and run her estate herself, making Darcy's younger children her heirs.

And for the best and last of it, to Elizabeth, he remained a steadfast husband, passionate, affectionate, and considerate of her feelings. For he counted his blessings in knowing that he achieved the very essence of what his heart desired. He had found true love. And may that be said of all of us, at some point in our lives.

And, as Elizabeth Bennet observed every Christmas-time, 'For what was lost was found, making it the most wonderful time of the year'.

The End

Afterword

Merry times, Reader. Merry times!

Thank you very much for picking up this novel and being up for another adventure of mine.

While a person can never live up to the genius writing of Jane Austen, and the timeless Christmas classic by Charles Dickens, this is a dream of mine that I had thought of for years.

By Darcy being in the place of Scrooge, there was a difficulty.

The chief problem for why I could never attempt it until now was that the 'Pride and Prejudice' concept clashed with the ghostly little book in one respect: Darcy had always been wealthy and had loving parents.

With Scrooge, he came from an apprenticeship, a hard childhood, much isolation, and his pursuit of wealth turned him into a 'scraping, covetous, old sinner'.

Therefore, came the beginning of how it could be achieved:

Miser to Misanthrope

While Scrooge is both a miser and a misanthrope, the first would not do for this tale, but the second easily could. Misanthrope, by definition, is a person who dislikes humankind and avoids human society.

Scrooge had misanthropic tendencies, and Darcy could easily channel them, especially if he was suffering from the disappointment of losing the love of his life. That would drive him to a state of bitterness that would make him want to retreat from the world.

Now, while one could never suspect that Darcy would let romantic loss affect him to such a degree that he would fall away from humanity, it is possible. His loss, mingled with knowing that he sacrificed his chief source of happiness for no reason at all, could afflict him mentally.

The transformation would be slow, but it could easily occur, from even the strongest of wills.

A tale Through Flashback

Due to the structure of 'A Christmas Carol', this story had to begin at the end of many events, and the love story had to be told through flashback. As such, certain events that would lead up to the building up of love, and the breaking down of the love, would be implied. The focus would be on the highlights of the rise and downfall of the romance.

And then there is Darcy and Elizabeth's reunion.

While it would seem natural to have their romance blossom soon after seeing each other again, and there be an exchange of pretty words, I didn't feel such.

In this tale, Elizabeth has been married and lost her husband in Britain's war in New Zealand. She is a widow, no longer has her parents, has learned to overcome tragedy, is enduring on her own, and has gained even more wisdom over the years. I do not think that time had diminished her wit and charisma, but only strengthened it, because she believes in perseverance.

Thus, she had the opposite reaction to Darcy's, when they had been separated.

He had wealth, but money could not buy him happiness.

She did not have much at all, so she had learned how to endure, and keep moving on. Their 'life-after-love' took different turns, but they still loved each other, through it all. And they complimented each other, in that manner.

Because of such, I believe that Elizabeth would have been strengthened over time. As such, when she saw Darcy again, she was going to be neither coy nor hesitant, or reserved. She would address the issue, straight on, wholly unafraid, unwilling to submit to a scripted way to approach the matter, and just be herself.

That fearlessness, mixed with her wit and inclination to tease Darcy, would bring about a mixture of humor, seriousness, wickedness, levity, depth, and heartfelt gut-wrenching emotion. It would have all those unconventional things because Darcy and Elizabeth's romance was anything but conventional.

A Tale of Romance & Family

While part of the focus on my books is romance, there is also a great focus on family as well, in them. That is why the book ended with seeing Georgiana again, rather than a wedding, because another vital aspect of Darcy's journey was to reunite with his sister. By him coming to see her, accepting her marriage, not only did he find completion on both sides, but he also did something that marked the end of his mistakes and the completion of his change. I hope the reader can understand my fascination with the focus on family. It brings more elements to these sorts of tales.

My favorite Versions of 'A Christmas Carol'

Dicken's classic novella is a gorgeous book that captures the essence of Christmastime and is impossible to grow old.

How many dramatized versions of the book are out there and we still keep coming back for more? Always.

It is a brilliant book by an accomplished author (though, I do not deny that I despise how Dickens treated his wife. But I can separate an artist from the art they create.) Each time that I read the story, I fall in love with it all over again.

While the story also makes a wonderful play to watch at a theatre, tv and film has captured the tale beautifully as well.

While I admit that I still have yet to see 'Spirited' and Barbie's 'A Christmas Carol', (despite what you think, the barbie movies can be quite entertaining, especially if you have children), I have a list.

I shall only list my favorite adaptations that have been faithful to the source material:

- A Christmas Carol, starring George C. Scott
- Scrooge, starring Albert Finney
- Scrooge/A Christmas Carol, starring Alistair Sims
- A Muppet's Christmas Carol
- A Christmas Carol (the animated one starring Tim Curry as Scrooge. It's quaint and I love it)
- A Christmas Carol, starring Patrick Stewart

Mind you, I still love 'A Christmas Carol' starring Jim Carrey a lot. And I very much appreciate 'Scrooge' Starring Sir Seymour Hicks. Even though it's older, the direction is good and Hicks played a wonderful Scrooge. The only thing that knocked it out of a spot was that I wish that we saw Marley's Ghost, and I felt Christmas Present could have been better. Also, I do like the television movie 'An American Christmas Carol', which is very well done, and 'A Diva's Christmas Carol' is a guilty pleasure. Ebony Scrooge is also a delight.

What can I say? I have plural tastes in things.

What is your favorite version?

Always remember, nothing is more fun than making a list.

Reader, thank you so much again, and I hope you enjoy whatever time of the year that you read this, for whatever time, it is a wonderful one.

Cheers!
Ney Mitch

THANK YOU FOR READING

Did you enjoy this book?

We invite you to leave a review at your favorite book site, such as Goodreads, Amazon, Barnes & Noble, etc.

DID YOU KNOW THAT LEAVING A REVIEW...

- Helps other readers find books they may enjoy.
- Gives you a chance to let your voice be heard.
- Gives authors recognition for their hard work.
- Doesn't have to be long. A sentence or two about why you liked the book will do.

About the Author

Ney Mitch has been a long-standing Jane Austen enthusiast, having written forty novels that were inspired by her various works. Since stumbling on Miss Austen's books after graduating from college, she has always dabbled in Austen inspired literature, ranging from writing works for teens to adults. Originally, her desire was to adapt Jane Austen's writing in a way to help young adults connect with her, however over time, she has spread her aims to other genres and styles. Having received her BA Degree at Desales University, she is a writer, both literary and dramatic, as well as being a Historic Reenactor.

 facebook.com/courtney.mitchell.589

X x.com/CMMitchelPsyche

P pinterest.com/shebaanna

Also by Ney Mitch

WITH SATIN ROMANCE

Austen Gaskell Series

Curiosities & Contemplation

Resolved & Resigned

Triumph & Tragedy

Woes & Worries

Love & Labors Won (Coming soon!)

Kitty Bennet Adventure Series

Vanities and Vexations

Forms & Fashions

Romance & Recklessness

Nuance & Novelty

Doubts & Difficulties

Follies & Forgiveness

Joys & Judgements

Romance & Revolution Saga

The First Impression

The Memory Series

Moments of Moments Past

Moments of Moments Present

Moments of Moments Future

Moments of Moments Infinite

Pride & Prejudice Reimaginings

Rapture & Rebellion

Fortune & Misfortune

Desire & Destiny

Pride & Peace

Resolve & Revelations

Hope & Hopelessness

Faith & Family

Seasonal Situations

Considearations Near Christmastime

Curiosities at Christmastime

Chances Series

Chances Are

Chances Come

Chances Fade

Chances End

<u>Novels</u>

The Tale of Mr. & Mrs. Bennet: A Pride & Prejudice Christmas Tale

The Wonderful Time of the Year